TOONOPOLIS:

Gemini

Toonopolis Files, Book One

by
Jeremy Rodden

Illustrated by Cami Woodruff

Published by Portmanteau Press LLC, Chesapeake, VA

Published by:
Portmanteau Press LLC
PO BOX 1411
Chesapeake, VA 23327
http://www.portmanteaupress.com/

ISBNs: 978-0-615-45721-5 (hardcover), 978-0-9834253-9-7 (paperback), 978-0-9834253-8-0 (eBook)

Cover art and design by:
Cami Woodruff
http://www.camiwoodruff.com/
Cover lettering by:
Jennifer Bruck

To my wonderful wife, Samantha: my best friend, my partner, and the unfortunate test subject for many bad jokes.

Contents

Prologue

Agent Log: Project Gemini
Entry Number: 1
Date: April 15

When I first returned from my trip to Toonopolis, I found it hard to put into words what I had experienced. I worried that the story about my time in the cartoon world would be seen, at best, as an excuse for failing a mission; at worst, as the rambling delusions of an agent who had lost his mind.

To this day, I still struggle when trying to explain my experiences. Fortunately for me, my superiors were not men to dismiss extraordinary tales easily, and my track record with the Agency was otherwise pristine. I reported to those stoic men just as I had done thousands of times before-

specific, detailed, chronological, and truthful.

At first, I simply hoped they believed me. After I completed my report, my feelings shifted to a hope that they wouldn't have me exterminated as an insane liability. If it were not for the possibility that this avenue might open doors to a new realm of opportunity for the Agency, they probably would have. I am just lucky that they were willing to take risks.

Based on my report, they funded Project Gemini. After initially fearing that my life was in jeopardy, I found myself leading a venture for the Agency that placed us at the genesis of a new era of covert operations.

The Agency spent millions of dollars and thousands of man-hours in the attempt to recreate the conditions that led to my entrance into the cartoon world, the Tooniverse, as the natives called it. It wasn't until we tapped into the resources of our neurology division that we realized

Prologue

we already possessed the requisite knowledge.

Though he didn't know it at the time, renowned neuroscientist Dr. James Robert Grenk had already discovered the process that could send someone into the Tooniverse. His research into a pain disorder known as RSD gave us the key, and his family yielded us a keymaster in his sixteen-year-old son. Jacob Grenk is a perfect test subject for us—intelligent, creative, and antisocial. Aside from his father, Jacob has no real meaningful connections to anyone.

After a year of research, development, and preparation, we are finally prepared to show my superiors that their judgment was not lacking and their trust in me was well-placed. Today we send a human consciousness into the Tooniverse to do our bidding.

Special Agent Mimic
April 15

Chapter One

Field Of Dreams

A teenage boy suddenly appeared in a field, his brow wrinkled in confusion. He was definitely stunned. In his left ear, he heard a faint popping sound followed by a slight whoosh of air as if an untied balloon had been released.

He unsuccessfully tried to remember anything prior to finding himself seated in this grassy field. He felt lost and confused and he realized that he was sitting down. He stood up, straightened his glasses, then brushed the clinging grass and dirt from his pants, and rubbed his hands together to remove the rest of the debris. He gazed around but could see nothing save the wide-open field in front of him.

It was a fortunate coincidence that an antique-style, full-length mirror walked up to him at that instant. The mirror gave him a full view of his reflection, even though he didn't recognize the boy he saw, a teenager, no more than fifteen or sixteen, with short unruly red hair and black horn-rimmed glasses. Freckles dotted his cheeks just below his cloudless blue eyes. The boy brought his pale, skinny arms to his face to ensure that he could feel what he was seeing and to confirm that it truly was his own image in the mirror.

He observed the gaudy clothes he was wearing— a lime green t-shirt and fuchsia cargo pants. He quickly recalled that the mirror in which he was examining himself had *walked* up to him. Even in his disoriented state of mind, he knew that mirrors couldn't just walk around wherever they wanted. At least, he thought he knew that.

"Hello?" the teenager said to the person he presumed was holding the mirror. He attempted to walk around to the back of the looking glass to see who was quietly taunting him. The mirror, though, spun with him to keep the reflective surface facing forward. "This isn't very funny, you know," the boy said

Much to the young man's surprise, the top portion of the mirror opened like a mouth and responded, "It also isn't very funny to try to look at someone else's butt without at least introducing yourself first." The looking glass emphasized its apparent disgust with a firm nod of the top of its frame.

"How are you doing that?" asked the boy, still trying to look behind the tall mirror.

"Well, if you are that interested in my backside, fine!" the mirror said in annoyance. It turned around, giving the red-haired boy a full view of a dark wooden backboard, such as one would expect to see on the reverse side of a tall looking glass. The mirror turned back around. "Are you satisfied?" it asked. Then it turned its back toward the bewildered boy again and began walking away on its very tiny legs.

The teenager looked down at his hands and back up to the mirror that was hobbling away as fast as its short legs would allow. "Wait," the boy whimpered quietly without really expecting the mirror to hear him. He had a million questions running through his mind but was unable to vocalize any of them. He paused to take an inventory of what information he had to work with to figure out where he was.

Before he could begin, the mirror was back in his face, showing the boy how much his forehead was crimpled in confusion. "Wait for what?" the looking glass asked, tapping one of its legs impatiently.

"Where am I?" was the question that jumped out of the boy's mouth. He didn't even have time to wonder how the mirror could hear him since it had no discernible ears.

"How should I know?" the mirror retorted. "I'm just an antique looking glass."

The young man suddenly had an idea inspired by a story from his childhood about a young girl who, like himself, found herself in a strange land full of bewilderment. It was with this thought in mind that he decided to run headfirst into the mirror. A loud *thud* and his rump landing on the grass were all he earned for his bright idea.

"Ow!" shouted the mirror. "What in the world did you do that for?"

"I guess I can't travel through you, huh?" The boy rubbed his head. He rose to his feet gingerly.

"I'm not sure why you thought you could. If you're quite done, I'd like to be on my way."

"On your way where?"

The boy thought he could make out annoyance in the upper frame of the looking glass, but he still couldn't figure out how it spoke. "Why, to Toonopolis, of course! It's where all of us begin our journeys."

The mirror spoke as though it was common knowledge. The young man wrinkled his brow with a grimace that clearly showed his ignorance of this information. "What is your name?" asked the mirror.

"I don't know."

"What an ill-formed thought you are," the mirror began. "You don't recall anything of your name or who you are?"

There was what seemed like a long pause as the boy struggled to come up with something that might be his name. He had plenty of vague memories floating in his mind, like the one about the girl and the looking glass, but to him it seemed that the only real existence he had ever known began moments ago when he became aware that he was sitting down in a field.

Only one word seemed to be a common thread in all of the jumbled memories that he was not sure were even his own. "Gemini," he said more to himself than to the mirror still standing impatiently in front of him.

"That's your name, kid? Gemini?"

Field of Dreams

"Kid . . . Gemini?" he mumbled, still mulling through his murky mind.

"Well, Kid Gemini—"

"No, just Gemini."

"Okay, Gemini," the annoyed mirror said. "I'm on my way to the big city. You can sit here and look dumb all you want, but I've got things to view and people to, er, view themselves." The mirror wobble-walked itself away from the boy.

"Gemini," he said out loud to test the name on his own ears. He wasn't entirely sure it actually was his name, as it did not sound very real to him. Then again, he thought, it was about as real as a walking, talking, standing mirror.

He decided to accept Gemini as his moniker. He felt good to have at least come up with a name for himself. The name alone did not, however, come close to answering the question of who he was, how he ended up in this strange field, or why he didn't clearly remember anything before the field.

While thinking about what he didn't know, the boy looked over the top of the retreating mirror and saw the large city on the horizon. As his gaze swept over the completely foreign city skyline, his eyes fell on the sun overlooking it.

Normally, the phrase "sun overlooking" would be an overused personification. In this case, however, the yellow-orange sun that Gemini was staring at actually had eyes and was quite literally looking at the city. Feeling the heat of Gemini's gaze, the sun turned its attention to the lone figure standing in the grass.

Gemini suddenly felt very small. When the sun winked at him, he nearly passed out. Gemini gaped at the cartoonish sun until the large ball of gas lost interest and turned its attention back toward the city. Gemini followed the sun's lead and also looked at the city skyline.

While there were some elements that reminded him of cityscapes he knew he had seen somewhere else before, there were also elements that reminded him of nothing he had seen before. He was not sure if it was because the city seemed so odd or if it was because his memory was so hazy.

Gemini saw tall skyscrapers made of glass, metal, wood, stone, and countless other materials, and could have sworn that one large building resembled a papier-mâché piñata. There also were numerous statues and monuments, some of which resembled ones he knew existed in other places. Some were completely new to him.

It was most difficult trying to absorb the vast diversity of the city he was looking at because it was constantly changing. Buildings were switching places, some of the monuments completely vanished only to be replaced by something new, and several of the buildings were changing colors, sizes, and even the construction materials right before his very eyes.

Gemini stood in the field trying to take in all he saw. He realized that he could not see an end to the city in either direction. The entire horizon at the edge of the field was covered with this shifting, varied cityscape.

"What is that?" he wondered aloud.

A loud popping sound next to him distracted Gemini. He turned toward the sound to find a large creature that appeared to be a cross between a kangaroo and a duck standing in a previously unoccupied space. The kangaroo-duck was wearing a yellow vest, a yellow sombrero, and nothing else. The creature looked like a five-year-old had drawn it.

"Hello?" Gemini ventured.

"Hola con queso!" screamed the kangaroo-duck and sprinted toward the city. After about fifty yards, the kangaroo-duck suddenly disappeared, leaving Gemini scratching his head and wondering if stranger things were even possible at this point.

Not knowing what else to do, he started walking toward the ever-changing city in the distance. As Gemini walked in the open field, he became aware of a path that he was fairly certain was not there when he began.

The rainbow-colored walkway was made of oddly shaped rectangular rocks with rounded edges. Or so he thought. He knelt down for a closer inspection and found the pathway to be made of a plethora of PEZ candies.

"Follow the Rainbow-PEZ Road," said a cheery voice behind him.

Gemini turned and discovered a being that resembled a garden gnome, who was smiling at him. The teenager thought his own fuchsia and lime clothing was gaudy, but the gnome made Gemini's clothes look plain in comparison. He was decked head to toe in rainbow-colored clothing including a giant bow tie and a pointy hat that looked like an old-school dunce cap.

"And who are you?" asked Gemini.

"My name is Roy," answered the gnome, his smile never faltering. "And you are?"

"Confused."

"Well, nice to meet you, Confused."

"No, my name isn't Confused. I'm confused."

Roy continued to smile, but his eyes narrowed a little. "Well, now I'm confused."

Gemini slapped himself in the face and groaned. "My name is Gemini. I am confused because I don't know what is going on and all of a sudden I find myself standing in a strange field talking to a garden gnome dressed in rainbows."

"Ah," said Roy, "I can see how that could be confusing."

Gemini sighed and stepped onto the Rainbow-PEZ Road with a loud crunch as the miniscule candy bricks crumbled under his sneakers. A wooden sign popped up in front of him as soon as his feet touched the road. He looked at Roy, who was still wearing a beaming smile.

"And which way should I follow this road?" asked Gemini.

"Read the sign," said Roy, the smiling gnome.

Gemini looked at the sign, which had a crudely drawn arrow on it pointing toward the large city at the end of the field and words written above the arrow: Toonopolis – 202,752 PEZes northeast. Just below that direction was an arrow pointing away from the road with the following words: Field of Dreams – 0 PEZes that-a-way.

Thanks to the timely intrusion of the magically appearing sign and Roy the gnome's encouragement, Gemini knew that the city he was walking toward was the same Toonopolis mentioned earlier by the mirror whose name he failed to catch.

"Well, I hope you learn a lot! Maybe we'll meet again one day!" Roy called out with more optimism than Gemini felt was healthy. He then vanished in an explosion of color that made Gemini shield his eyes.

Gemini turned away from the spot where the gnome had been standing and began his crunching, PEZ-dust-creating trek toward the city in the distance. He eyed the Rainbow-PEZ Road as it cut a colorful line in the otherwise plain green field around him.

He moved closer to Toonopolis, occasionally picking up handfuls of PEZ to eat along the way. He could only imagine what would await him inside the city limits. Gemini munched on the road and he knew his journey was bound to get even more interesting before he had any answers to who he really was and why he was in this weird place.

Chapter Two

Sorting Square

Shortly before he reached the arched entranceway into the city, Gemini fell in with a throng of the most miscellaneous collection of people, creatures, and animals that he could possibly imagine. After having his foot stepped on by a centaur's cloven hoof, he nearly got knocked off the road by a wayward swinging sack belonging to a cat burglar. The sack carried by the human thief was meowing and had sharp claws poking through the burlap.

"NEXT!" a booming voice yelled from the front of the motley crowd. Gemini was amazed that he was able to even make out such a distinct sound over the tumult of noise surrounding him.

Gemini strained to look over the shoulders of the taller members of the crowd to see what manner of being created such a large noise. His eyes focused on a mammoth man with long stringy black hair, who reminded him of a pro wrestler. "NEXT!" he heard again, but the shout did not come from the wrestler.

The crowd continued to push forward as Gemini heard the loud voice over and over again. The group steadily dissipated as each member stepped forward in front of the wrestler, who pointed various directions to each creature that stood before him. As he got closer, Gemini saw a microphone. He guessed it stood around a foot tall on little legs propping it up. "NEXT!" the microphone shouted. It wasn't until the cat burglar nudged him that Gemini realized it was his turn.

"Name?" asked the wrestler in an unlikely high-pitched voice that emphasized the irony of the duo sorting the crowd.

"Uh, Gemini," he replied with minimal confidence.

"Genre?"

Gemini simply stared at the wrestler dumbfounded. "What?" he queried.

"What genre are you?" the annoyed wrestler repeated.

"I don't know. I'm just a boy."

The wrestler shrugged and looked at the microphone. "Mike, we have ourselves a confused one here."

"Well, Michael," said Mike at a quieter volume than his previous shouts, "that means one of two things: an ill-conceived idea or an Outsider. Send him to the master sorter. He'll figure it out."

Returning to his full height after crouching to confer with his partner, the wrestler pointed to his right. Gemini followed his finger, which directed him to a cloaked figure standing inside a window that very much resembled a fast food drive-through. Not having any other options, the boy walked up to the window.

His head was swirling with a million thoughts ever since he mysteriously appeared in the Field of Dreams on the outskirts of the city. He was hopeful that this "master sorter" would be able to answer some of them. Gemini felt that his experiences were much too real to be a dream. Also, he was fortunate to still be young enough to accept the extraordinary.

"A difficult ssssort, eh?" hissed the cloaked figure at the drive-through. "Let's ssssee what those two couldn't." The figure pulled back the emerald green cloak, revealing yellow eyes with black vertical slits embedded in a reptilian face covered with green and yellow scales. Gemini immediately felt that this creature could see more than just his physical body with those eyes.

"What are you?" Gemini blurted out. Accepting or not, he was reaching a point where he needed some answers, and the intelligence in the yellow eyes suggested that the reptile might have some answers for him.

"I am a draconid, youngling, but that doessss not matter. What matters issss what you are."

"I'm a human boy. I thought that was obvious."

"In the Tooniverse, nothing is obvioussss, boy," the draconid snapped at Gemini. "Nothing is what it sssseems to be. What sort of cartoon are you?" The question seemed to be rhetorical, but Gemini froze at the word "cartoon."

"I'm a cartoon?" Gemini asked.

"Yessss," the creature answered nonchalantly. "You don't sssseem to be ill-conceived, but you also don't seem to be complete either." The draconid had begun leaning closer to Gemini, but the red-haired boy didn't notice.

Gemini suddenly sprang back to himself and noticed that the master sorter's face was within a few inches of his own. He took a quick step backwards and put his hands up. "What are you doing?" he demanded.

"I have the power to ssssee into each creation and determine its purposssse."

"You know," Gemini changed the subject, "that hissing is really getting annoying. And you're spitting on me."

"Oh, ssssorry," started the sorter. He reached a scaly hand into his mouth and pulled out a retainer. "I just woke up and I left in my retainer. Sorry about that." Gemini shook his head in exasperation. "As I was saying, I can see into each creation and sort it to its proper place in Toonopolis. Most of the time, it is easy to determine based on appearance. You pose a problem, however."

"And how is that?"

"You are incomplete, for one. And," the draconid started pensively, "you don't seem to be a creation at all. You must be an Outsider."

Gemini put his hand to his chin and tried to take in what the draconid sorter was telling him.

He thought about suddenly appearing in the field outside and the strange interaction with the walking, talking looking glass. He thought about his trek upon the Rainbow-PEZ Road and the strange gnome named Roy. He attempted to put all the pieces together along with what the scaly creature was saying.

Finally, he said, "Yeah, you lost me."

The scaly green sorter sighed and shook his head. "I figured as much. Most Outsiders are lost. That's why we give them an aide when they first arrive. I'd love to stay here all day and answer your inane questions, but the crocodile down the street just laid a half dozen eggs and I am starving." The draconid pulled his hood up and began to close the window.

"Wait!" cried Gemini. "Where do I get an aide? Who can answer my questions? What do you mean when you say 'Outsider'?" Gemini fired off questions as quickly as he could until the draconid leaned down inside his window and threw an oblong purple object at him.

As the object thumped into Gemini, both he and the purple item screamed. Gemini picked up the object that the draconid so casually threw at him. "Holy cow!" he shouted as he noticed a face on the front of it, causing him to drop it on the ground.

** 20 **

Sorting Square

"Ow," mumbled the purple thing as it righted itself. Gemini stepped back to get a better look at it and noticed that he was staring at an oversized eggplant with two large eyes and a big smiling mouth. It had no arms or legs that he could see, but it was able to balance itself on its rounded bottom. "Well, that was fun."

"Sorry about that," Gemini began. "I wasn't expecting the sorter to throw a talking eggplant at me. Why did he do that?"

"'Cause he's a jerk," the talking eggplant declared. "Allow me to introduce myself: Jimbob the Talking Eggplant." Jimbob made a little bow as he gave his name. "I will be your aide to the Tooniverse. You're my first assignment so be patient with me, willya?"

"I'm Gemini, I think. I'm your first assignment? How long have you been here?" he asked.

"That's a hard question to answer, kid. Time doesn't move here like it does on Earth."

Gemini frowned. "Well, what day is it? What year is it?"

"It's Saturday morning," the eggplant answered succinctly. Gemini began to ask another question, but Jimbob interrupted him. "It's always Saturday morning in Toonopolis. Time neither stands still nor does it move here. It just is. Maybe we should start with a simpler question."

"Fine. What's with the whole 'sorting' thing? What did the draconid mean when he called me an Outsider? And he called me a cartoon. What's that all about? Why am I incomplete?" Gemini's mouth couldn't keep up with his mind's racing questions.

Jimbob looked up at his new charge. "Let's go sit down and have something to eat. I'll explain as best as I can." Jimbob bounced away from the drive-through window area and toward a restaurant with tables set up outside in a good place to view the Sorting Square. The microphone and wrestler were still NEXTing and pointing to the myriad creatures meandering their way into the square from the Field of Dreams.

A wooden sign hung above the doorway to the restaurant with a painted pair of binoculars and Sortview Inn painted underneath. Gemini figured that he knew how the restaurant got its name.

Jimbob the Talking Eggplant ordered two chocolate milks with bendy straws, which the waiter produced almost immediately. Jimbob took a sip of his milk and began his explanation, "You see, kid, you're in the cartoon world, the Tooniverse. The short version is that this universe is where all of the thoughts and ideas of sentient beings in the regular universe live."

"Sentient beings? You mean humans?" Gemini ventured.

Jimbob smiled. "Not entirely. Humans make up most of the sentient beings in the universe, yes. But they are not the only ones. Didn't you ever watch The X-Files? Humans aren't even the only beings on Earth that can think abstractly." Jimbob shook his head and mumbled to himself, "If only people didn't denounce Douglas Adams as merely a fiction writer." He shrugged off the thought. "Regardless, that's what makes up this world, for the most part."

Gemini stared at the eggplant and slurped the remnants at the bottom of his glass. He didn't realize that he had forgotten to breathe while drinking his chocolate milk until he began sucking in air.

Jimbob laughed at him. "I know it sounds crazy, but the Tooniverse is just as real as the universe you came from."

Gemini found his voice. "So I'm just an idea?"

"Let's not get all existential here, Gemini. You are a cartoon, yes, but you are different from the creations you see all around you. At least, according to Henry, the master sorter."

"His name is Henry?"

"I guess he didn't introduce himself, huh?" said Jimbob. "You figured he'd have some sort of made-up fantasy name, being a mystical creature? Well, some beings aren't too creative when it comes to naming their creations. But back on track, you are different because you are not a creation. You are a real human, transported here in cartoon form—an Outsider."

If Gemini thought the idea of being a creation was hard to swallow, the thought that he was an actual human who had somehow entered the Tooniverse as a cartoon was even more surreal.

"Why don't I remember anything before the Field of Dreams?"

"That's a little harder for me to answer," Jimbob said. "Most Outsiders can't handle the reality of the Tooniverse and just go insane. Rare is the Outsider who can handle the sudden jolt to his awareness that existence is even greater than the universe proper." Gemini stared at the purple vegetable in front of him and tried to take in all that he was saying. "It might have something to do with your incompleteness that Henry mentioned."

Gemini started to ask another question, but Jimbob held up a purple hand to stop him. "Before you ask, I have no idea what he meant by that, but clearly you're missing parts of your memory and therefore, parts of yourself."

Gemini thought for a moment while a humanoid waitress refilled both his and Jimbob's glasses of chocolate milk. "Wait, where did that hand come from? You don't have hands."

"Well, as Henry said, nothing in the Tooniverse is as obvious as it seems. I have hands when I need them, just as most cartoons can have whatever they need when they need them. But that's a whole new lesson best saved for another day." Jimbob leaned in and drank some of his milk. "As for your first question about the sorting—"

"NEXT!" they heard the microphone shout.

"Toonopolis is chaotic by nature. I'm sure you noticed that by now." Jimbob smiled a knowing smile. "Mike daFone and Michael Djin over there help organize the constant influx of new toons. Toonopolis is organized into an ever-changing and ever-growing number of sections based on the genre in which each toon fits. They're free to travel between districts, but most toons feel more comfortable in their home district."

"What's an ill-conceived?"

"An incomplete thought. They're real enough to exist but not complete enough to stick around. They get thrown into a bottomless pit."

Gemini gasped and stared wide-eyed at the eggplant.

"I'm just kidding!" Jimbob laughed. "They just get put aside. Most of the time they simply vanish as quickly as they appeared. The majority of them never even make it past the Field of Dreams."

Gemini thought back to the kangaroo-duck he saw in the Field of Dreams that disappeared as it ran toward the city. He understood what Jimbob was telling him. There was a long pause in silence as the young man and the talking eggplant looked at each other over their tall frosty glasses of chocolate milk.

Gemini felt that quite a bit of time passed as they listened to the sounds of the sorting going on in the square. Then he remembered that time didn't operate the same way in the Tooniverse as it did in the universe.

"So," he began, "now what?"

"Well, that's up to you. You're an Outsider. There's a lot of power that comes along with that if you can harness it properly. You can try to find a way home if you want, but you'll probably have to figure out how to complete yourself first. I'd hate to see what happens to an incomplete Outsider who finds his way home."

"A quest?"

"Or a journey. However you want to look at it. Either way, my job is to be your guide."

"Like my conscience?"

Jimbob whistled and said, "Just call me Jiminy Cricket, kid."

Gemini laughed. "I guess it's time for an adventure. Any suggestions on where we should begin?"

Jimbob hopped onto his bottom from the chair, a broad grin on his face. "If we're going questing, there's only one place to start!"

"Where would that be?"

"You're a young man about to start a quest that is clearly beyond your age and capabilities," Jimbob said with an enthusiasm that made Gemini a little leery. "We've got to start in the Adventure Realm!"

With that suggestion, Jimbob hopped away from the restaurant with Gemini struggling to keep pace. He didn't stop to wonder why neither of them had to pay at the restaurant; he was too excited to begin his journey.

Chapter Three

Adventure Realm

Jimbob the Talking Eggplant led Gemini to a section of Toonopolis that very much resembled a quaint little farm town. There were sounds of a blacksmith hammering in his shop and the bleating of sheep and goats penned nearby.

Gemini looked across the dirt road in front of him and wondered how the city had changed so drastically from Sorting Square. The buildings here were all made of wood, and dust hung in the air all around the town. He saw a sign painted with a baby pig hanging above a building. There was a roasted apple shoved into the pig's mouth.

"Ah," said Jimbob, "the Suckling Pig. That's where we want to go."

Gemini was hesitant. "I'm just a teenager, Jimbob. Why would I want to go to a bar?"

Jimbob had already begun hopping across the dirt street toward the Suckling Pig. There was music streaming through the tavern's open door that sounded like it came from crude string and wind instruments. "It's not a bar. It's a tavern. And you want to go there because nearly every quest starts at one. Maybe we can find something to help make you complete!"

Grudgingly, Gemini followed his guide across the dusty road and through the Suckling Pig's swinging front doors. The boy looked around at the nearly empty tavern and spotted a few drunken men at the bar along with some very unenthused looking minstrels playing their medieval instruments by the fire.

A barmaid looked up from the wooden table she was wiping down and her eyes lit up. "Are you the chosen one?" she asked in Gemini's direction.

"Am I the what?" he responded, baffled.

"The chosen one. Why else would a teenager walk into a tavern unless he were the chosen one?" The barmaid moved closer to Gemini as she spoke.

Gemini glanced over at Jimbob, who appeared to be enjoying the spectacle very much. "I told you I shouldn't be here, Jimbob." Gemini turned to leave the Suckling Pig.

Jimbob stopped his retreat and spoke to the barmaid, "No, m'lady, he is not your chosen one. He is a fresh young adventurer looking to make a name for himself by slaying and killing and all of that good stuff." Jimbob bowed to the barmaid. He glanced up at Gemini with a mischievous look and winked at him.

"Oh, you've got to be kidding me!" Gemini threw up his arms as he pushed past Jimbob and walked out of the tavern.

He made it two steps out the door when Jimbob came bouncing up behind him, laughing hysterically. "I'm sorry, kid, but that was just too much fun. Seriously, though, I talked to the barmaid and she showed me a list posted in the tavern for adventurers."

"I don't see how that helps me." Gemini sulked.

"Well, we don't have any other leads. Maybe if we pick one of these quests, we'll get lucky."

Jimbob held out a piece of paper. "I like the first one."

Gemini turned to face Jimbob and snatched the paper out of his hand, saying, "Let me see that sheet." He read aloud the first quest on the list. "'Questgiver: Barmaid Hanna. Reward: Ten silver. Quest: Slay five giant rats in the cellar of the Suckling Pig.'"

He put down the paper and looked at Jimbob, who was literally rolling on the ground with laughter. "If an eggplant pees himself, what color is it?" he asked his vegetable guide.

Jimbob immediately stopped laughing and looked hurt. "Okay, so I guess you don't like that one. What about the next one?"

Gemini returned to reading the second quest on the list. "'Questgiver: Chi Lin. Reward: The undying gratitude of the last real unicorn. Quest: Locate Chi Lin's maiden, Avantika, who was kidnapped by an unknown assailant.'"

"Oooh," mocked Jimbob, "'undying gratitude', eh? Let's kill the rats for silver instead!"

Gemini shook his head and read the third and last quest. "'Questgiver: The people of Adventure Realm. Reward: One hundred gold. Quest: A mysterious shadowy figure has been killing toons all over Toonopolis. He must be stopped.'" He sighed. "How am I supposed to deal with that? Besides, you can't kill toons, can you?"

Jimbob looked pensive for a moment. "Well, not by traditional means, no. At least, you can't permanently kill a cartoon."

"Well, how can you kill a toon then?" Gemini walked over to a bench in front of the tavern and watched a man on a horse walk past. "Maybe this whole quest thing was a bad idea."

At that moment, another young man, clad in a loose-fitting white tunic and brown linen pants, strode past Gemini and Jimbob as they talked. Gemini watched him walk confidently into the tavern. From inside, he could hear barmaid Hanna's screech, "Oh, you must be the chosen one!" Gemini rolled his eyes.

Jimbob hopped over to him and looked at the list. "Well, maybe we should see about that unicorn thing. They have magic. Maybe it can help us out."

Before Gemini could respond, the young man who had just entered the Suckling Pig came back out and stood facing him. "I'd like that quest list, please. Hanna tells me there are rats to be killed." He pulled out a wooden sword. "And I aim to kill them."

"You're going to kill them with that? You plan on smacking them to death?"

Jimbob jumped in to add, "And really, why is there a limit to how many she wants killed? Are there only five down there or is that just a random quota she set up?"

Gemini threw his hands up in the air and said, "This place is ridiculous."

Gemini crumpled up the quest list and threw it at the other young man's feet. As he stood, Gemini noticed that they were of equal height, but his counterpart had black hair and no glasses. This observation made Gemini adjust his glasses as he turned his back to the other boy.

"How dare you insult this fine tavern? I challenge you to a duel!" As he spoke, a giant flag fell from the sky and landed between Gemini and the other boy. "I am Leothas, the chosen one, and I will not stand idly by and allow you to belittle the importance of this quest."

"Okay, where did that flag come from? And what are you talking about? I'm not going to duel with you." Gemini turned his back on Leothas and started walking up the dirt road. Leothas ran at Gemini and thwacked him in the back of the head with his wooden sword. "Ow!" shouted Gemini. "What was that for?"

"En garde!" Leothas responded. "I have struck first. Now it is your turn."

Gemini rubbed the back of his head and faced his assailant. "What do you mean 'it is your turn?' Why would we take turns?" Before Leothas could answer, Jimbob the Talking Eggplant bounced to Gemini's side and handed him his own sword made out of wood.

"Why wood? Can't I just use a metal sword? I heard the blacksmith working over there." He pointed with his wooden sword at the blacksmith shop, still ringing with the sounds of hammers striking metal.

Jimbob shrugged. "The shopkeep was only selling wooden weapons. I asked her about metal ones, and she said you weren't high enough level to use metal yet."

"Enough talking," cried Leothas. "It is your turn."

Gemini smiled. "So, what you're saying is that you can't attack me again until I attack you? Some magical force is making this fight turn-based? What happens if I just don't attack you back?"

Leothas looked stunned. He retreated from his attacking stance into a thoughtful one. He had one hand on his hip and rubbed his chin with the other. "I don't know. I was always taught to take turns attacking. I don't know any other way to fight."

"Yeah, good luck with that." With a smirk, Gemini dropped his wooden sword into the dirt and walked up the road. "Come on, Jimbob, let's go ask some townfolk if they know anything about this shadowy figure. This place is making me feel dumber for having been here." Jimbob picked up the sword and bounced along behind Gemini.

"You get back here and take your turn, insolent scum! I am the chosen one and I say we must battle!" Leothas shouted as he receded more and more into the background.

Jimbob and Gemini rounded a corner and approached a new part of the town that seemed to serve as a meeting square. Several villagers were standing at a well, waiting to draw water.

"So what was that whole turn-taking thing about?" asked Gemini.

Jimbob responded, "It was an archaic form of fighting from early adventuring days. No one even uses it anymore unless they are fighting with strange looking creatures that fit inside a little ball in your pocket."

"What?"

"You know, pocket monsters."

Gemini stared at Jimbob and blinked a few times. He sighed and decided to just accept the explanation and move on.

The teenager moved closer to the villagers at the well. He approached a stout man with a brown bushy beard and mustache. "Excuse me, sir, do you know anything about this shadowy figure that has supposedly been killing people in Toonopolis?"

The man's eyes grew wide, and he dropped his bucket. It flipped as it fell and landed directly on top of Jimbob the Talking Eggplant. The bucket bounced around with muffled cries from Jimbob until he fell over and rolled down a slight decline and into a fence. Gemini ran to retrieve his guide, who had shrugged off the bucket and looked like he was going to throw up.

"Are you okay?" Gemini asked the eggplant.

"I think I was too short for that ride. That was very unsafe." Jimbob turned back to the bucket and heaved into it. The bearded villager approached and looked like he was out to retrieve his bucket but changed his mind as he watched a talking eggplant puke into it.

Gemini said to the villager, "So, do you have any information on the figure or not?" The man shook his head but was very unconvincing. Gemini could see the fear in his eyes that betrayed his true feelings. "Just tell me what you know. I am on a quest to stop him."

The villager gaped at Gemini and pointed a finger toward him. He opened his mouth to speak, but Gemini interrupted him. "If you call me the chosen one, I will dump this eggplant-spew-filled bucket on your head."

"I'll tell you what I know, lad," said the bearded man. He picked up his bucket, which made a sick sloshing sound. Jimbob stood up but looked unsteady. The villager motioned for Gemini and Jimbob to follow him a distance from the well out of earshot of the other townspeople.

"He's still in this town," the man whispered to Gemini.

Gemini and Jimbob exchanged excited glances. Gemini said, "Well, where? This might be the fastest one hundred gold ever made."

"He's over on the old McDonald farm."

Gemini stared at him and blinked. Jimbob the Talking Eggplant broke the silence by singing, "E I E I O!" At a nudge from Gemini, Jimbob took a more serious tone. "I wonder what kind of sound a shadowy figure makes."

"Just tell me where the farm is, please," Gemini requested of the villager. He was annoyed and wanted to get his quest over with. He highly doubted that this would help him get home, find out about himself, or otherwise have any usefulness, but Gemini wanted to complete the task all the same. It just felt like the right thing to do.

"It's just on the other side of the village, past the butcher, the baker, and the candlestick maker."

"Are they in a tub?" The villager looked at Gemini quizzically. "Never mind." He looked at Jimbob, who had finally regained his footing even though he had no visible feet.

Jimbob was preoccupied with trying to determine what sound a shadowy figure made. "Whooosh. Whoooo. Spooky spooky spooky." Jimbob looked up at Gemini. "I have no idea what sound a shadowy figure makes. I think we need a new animal. It's like when someone throws out 'kangaroo' at you. You try to say 'hop,' but kangaroos don't really say 'hop'."

"Are you quite finished?"

"Sure thing, boss. Let's go to the old McDonald farm. I want a happy meal."

"You are the worst guide ever."

"Probably."

Gemini thanked the villager and left him with the unenviable task of cleaning out eggplant vomit from his bucket. The boy and the purple vegetable traveled quickly to the other end of the village, passing by many townsfolk who acted like spooked horses when Gemini and Jimbob crossed their paths. As they passed the candlemaker's shop, Gemini saw a dilapidated farm that looked as though it hadn't had a farmhand work it for years.

"That farm didn't look like that a few days ago," said a young female voice behind Gemini and Jimbob.

Gemini jumped at the sudden sound. "Holy cow, lady!" he shouted. Gemini turned to face the speaker only to find a little girl with blond pigtails wearing a red and white checked sundress. "What do you mean? That farm looks like it's been abandoned for years."

Jimbob added, "And where's the picnic?" As the little girl and Gemini glared at him, he said, "Well, you know, because of the dress. Looks like a . . ." He got quieter. "A picnic table."

The pigtailed girl ignored Jimbob. "It was only a few days ago that the shadowy figure appeared at the farm. He's been absorbing the life of the farm."

"Absorbing the life?" asked Gemini.

"He just sucks it up. Cows, crops, people. He sucked it all up."

Jimbob made a little whimper. Gemini thought at first that he was scared. After a glance at his purple companion, he realized he was trying to hold his tongue. "Just get it out," Gemini said. Jimbob shook his head. "Come on, just say it."

"The shadowy figure sucks!" blurted Jimbob.

"Feel better?" Jimbob nodded his head, and Gemini turned back to the little girl. "Where is the figure now?"

She opened her mouth to answer, but Gemini interrupted her, "Wait, let me guess. Holed up in the barn?"

The girl was shocked. "How did you know?"

"Lucky guess." Gemini turned to Jimbob. "Let's get this thing over with."

Jimbob pulled the wooden sword from behind his back and handed it to his charge. "You don't want to go in unarmed, do you?"

"What am I going to do? Splinter him to death?" Still, he took the sword from the talking eggplant, and the two of them made their way through the deserted farm toward the barn on the far end of the field. The doors were falling off the hinges.

Gemini stepped inside. "Hello? Any shadowy figures in here?"

A throaty reply came from the hayloft above the stalls. "Get out," was all the voice said.

Jimbob the Talking Eggplant made an 'I've-got-this' motion to Gemini and stepped farther into the barn. He said in a falsetto voice, "We're selling cookies for our troop. Would you like to buy some?"

After a pause, the voice said, "Do you have the little chocolate minty ones?"

"No," replied Jimbob. "I'm sorry, but your neighbor bought the last box." Jimbob gave Gemini a quick thumbs-up motion as the two of them crept closer to the hayloft.

"In that case," the voice said, "DIE!" The shadowy figure leapt down from the hayloft straight at Jimbob the Talking Eggplant. Gemini quickly jumped in front of his purple compatriot, wooden sword in hand.

Gemini looked at the flying figure heading toward him. It was roughly human-shaped but Gemini couldn't see any of its features. He couldn't tell if it was smoke or shadows that obscured them or maybe it was a mixture of the two swirling around him. As the figure swooped, the shadows and smoke trailed behind it like a comet's tail.

The shadowy figure swarmed on top of Gemini, who swung his sword frantically. "I can't hit him! And I just got a splinter in my thumb! This wooden sword is useless." The shadowy figure enveloped Gemini, who began choking. He could not see anything except a swarm of black smoke surrounding him. He fell to his knees.

"You were not on my list, boy, but it is no matter. You shall be absorbed like the rest of them. You will die." Gemini gasped and fell to the ground.

He braced for death when the shadowy figure suddenly screamed in pain and dissipated, leaving Gemini gasping for air. A throaty voice let Gemini know that the figure was not gone even though the shadows and smoke had vanished. "What are you?" it asked rhetorically.

Jimbob bounded to Gemini's side as the young adventurer coughed and sputtered. "Are you okay, kid? What just happened?"

"So much pain. Too much. Can't handle it." Gemini breathed the words with much difficulty. The last things he remembered were Jimbob's questions, and more strongly, the throaty voice of the shadowy figure asking what he was. Then he blacked out.

Agent Log: Project Gemini
Entry Number: 5
Date: May 13

After several weeks of stability, there was a huge spike in Jacob's brain-wave activity yesterday. I was worried that we might be on the verge of losing him, but Dr. Viktor Kraft, a new assistant we brought in to work with Dr. Grenk, assures me that his brain-wave activity has already dipped back to normal levels.

Dr. Grenk gave me some story about only being able to monitor the physical body of his son and not his consciousness, but I am beginning to worry that his emotional ties to his son are clouding his judgment. His claim that the brain-wave activity increase could indicate that Jacob's "consciousness was being attacked" made no sense to me. I have been to the Tooniverse, and nothing there was capable of attacking an Outsider's consciousness.

Thankfully, several names on the list we gave our operative inside the Tooniverse have already been incapacitated. If it were not for that, we would have nothing tangible to prove to my superiors that we were being successful. Dr. Grenk has become more and more detached since we first sent his son's consciousness into the Tooniverse. He doesn't seem to be all there. Dr. Kraft's involvement has little to do with a lack of faith in Dr. Grenk's abilities and more to do with our fear that he may need to be removed from this project to avoid becoming a detriment to the operation.

Now that my superiors have seen how easy it is for our operatives in Project Gemini to infiltrate the very minds of the Agency's enemies, I feel confident in requesting additional funds to set up more Tooniverse agents. Grenk's son was an ideal candidate for this process to begin with, and now I feel it is time we pushed for more. At this rate, covert assassinations of the past will be rendered obsolete within a few months. I feel fortunate to be on the forefront of this endeavor. Only good things can come to the Agency from this exercise.

Special Agent Mimic
May 13

Chapter Four

Tooniversity

Gemini awoke in a hospital bed. He opened his eyes and looked down at his body, which had several wire leads running underneath his clothes and an IV in his left arm. Inexplicably, he was still wearing his lime green shirt and fuchsia pants. He assumed that he would have been stripped of his normal clothing and cloaked in a hospital gown by now. He guessed that hospitals in Toonopolis didn't work the same as they did on Earth.

A sudden observation hit his brain: he was still in the cartoon world. This jolt of realization made him sit up sharply. Jimbob the Talking Eggplant, who was sitting asleep on a chair next to Gemini's bed, awoke with a start. "You're awake, Gemini!"

"Yeah, Jimbob. How long have I been out?"

"Well, it's hard to say. Time . . ."

"Yeah, I know, time doesn't work here like it does on Earth. What happened to Shadowy Figure? How did I get here?"

Jimbob stood up on his chair to look at Gemini. "Hang on, Quizzy McQuesterson. I have a question for you first." Gemini waited and motioned for Jimbob to continue. "Before you passed out, you said something about 'too much pain.' What did the shadowy figure do to you?"

Gemini searched his memory. He realized then that his memory went back much further than the Field of Dreams. He remembered his life on Earth. He remembered his father, the important researcher who had more time for his work than for his son. He remembered being picked on at his high school for being a "weirdo." He remembered being brought into the Agency to test out his father's newest experiment.

"My memory is back!" he shouted.

Jimbob looked very excited and cheered. "All of it? You remember who you are?"

Gemini removed the IV from his arm and discovered that it was simply a taped-down tube and didn't actually have a needle penetrating his skin. He likewise found that the leads running to his body were just wires with no ends didn't monitor his life signs at all. He was quickly realizing that things in the Tooniverse were usually centered on appearing to be real instead of actually being real.

He tried to recall if he remembered everything. He felt there was still a gap. "I'm missing some time. I don't remember my time spent with the Agency. I remember showing up at the Agency's headquarters and then I remember the Field of Dreams."

"Wait, if you remember all of that, then you remember who you are!" Jimbob said hopefully.

"I do," Gemini muttered. A flood of emotions assailed him. He was excited to have his memory back. He also remembered that he was not very happy in his old life. There was also anger at his father, and he was still a bit confused.

He remembered his real name: Jacob Grenk. He thought about his father using him as a guinea pig for the Agency's project and about his abandonment inside the Tooniverse. Gemini did not want to live that life anymore. He looked up at Jimbob the Talking Eggplant and said, "I am Gemini."

Jimbob looked a little disappointed, but it seemed to Gemini that he was trying to hide it. "So then, you still don't know how you ended up in the Tooniverse?"

"Right, but I know it has something to do with the Agency and my father. I need to find Shadowy Figure. For whatever reason, when he tried to absorb me I got back a lot of my memories. I'm guessing I can get the rest back from him." A look of determination came across Gemini's face as he swung his legs over the side of the hospital bed and jumped to the floor.

Jimbob cocked his head to the side and asked, "Did you just call him Shadowy Figure? Like it was his name? Not *the* shadowy figure?"

Gemini shrugged. "Well, we don't know anything else about him. It seems like a good name to me."

Jimbob nodded and smiled at the young man. "It's questing time?"

"Oh, it's questing time all right. And we've got a smoke- and shadow-covered villain to track down."

Gemini let his adrenalin wind down a little bit and looked around. "You never answered my questions. Where are we and how did I get here?"

Jimbob hopped off his chair and came next to Gemini. "We're at Tooniversity Hospital. The villagers were so excited that you got rid of the shadowy figure from the Adventure Realm that they helped carry you here."

"I will have to thank them next time I am in Adventure Realm."

"Sure, but since we're here at the Tooniversity," he suggested, "maybe we should spend some time getting you educated on cartoon physics so you're better equipped to deal with the shadowy figure next time you face him."

"I already know a lot about cartoons. Now that I have my memory back, I remember that I used to spend a lot of time watching them."

Jimbob nodded. "Can't hurt to get some more lessons, though, right?"

"I guess you're right," Gemini conceded. "Let's go get some lessons on cartoon physics."

Gemini walked out of the hospital room, wondering why no nurse or doctor questioned his exit. As they walked the hallways, Gemini pondered who would be teaching lessons on cartoon physics. He voiced that thought to Jimbob.

"There's a rabbit and there's a mouse that teach most of the classes here," Jimbob said matter-of-factly.

Gemini stopped and stared, mouth agape, at Jimbob. "Are you talking about the Big Two? Bugs and Mickey?" He felt like a kid about to meet his favorite baseball player, or in this case, a boy about to meet his favorite cartoon characters.

Jimbob laughed. "No, not those two. They haven't been in Toonopolis in years. Not since they were young ideas."

Gemini looked disappointed but continued walking down the hall while firing questions at his Tooniverse guide. "Why are there no famous toons in Toonopolis? I know it's a big city, but I would have guessed I'd run into one of them at some point."

As Jimbob bounced alongside Gemini, struggling to keep up with the young man's pace, he attempted to explain. "Toonopolis is a place for individual ideas. Cartoons and worlds that have gained widespread acceptance become TMed."

"Trademarked?"

Jimbob shook his head. "Terminally moved," he corrected. "Places like Neverland, Narnia, and Wonderland were all parts of Toonopolis once. In Toonopolis, though, ideas belong only to one being. Once more beings accept the thoughts as their own, those thoughts get moved into other parts of the Tooniverse."

"So Toonopolis is kind of like a rest stop?"

"A rest stop that is the center of the Tooniverse, yeah."

"Could I travel to these TMed places if I wanted to?"

Jimbob thought for a moment. "Well, creations can't unless they get absorbed into one of those TMed worlds. Outsiders are different. I guess you could if you really wanted to. Not sure why you would, though. Those places aren't nearly as interesting as Toonopolis."

"Why not?"

"Toonopolis is constantly changing. The more well-known those other worlds are, the more rigid they become, like Tolkien's Middle Earth. Or they become mixed up with so many different minds involved that they don't even make sense anymore, like the Marvel Universe."

Gemini begrudgingly accepted the explanation. "Why are they called Terminally Moved?"

"Once something becomes the idea of more than one being, it can never return to Toonopolis. It either stays public domain or fades from memory. It can never belong just to the original creator again."

Jimbob stopped outside a wooden door with a translucent glass window. They could see the silhouette of a rabbit through the door. "Professor Rabbit: Physics 101" was printed in black block letters on the window. Jimbob knocked on the door.

"Come in," called a voice from inside. Gemini opened the door to find a brown rabbit erasing a chalkboard in front of an empty classroom. He wore a tweed jacket with leather patches on the elbows but nothing else.

"Hi, Professor Rabbit. I'm Jimbob the Talking Eggplant, guide to this Outsider, Gemini."

The rabbit spoke with a haughty accent as he responded, "Ah, splendid! An Outsider who didn't lose his mind coming into the Tooniverse? It's been some years since we've had one of those. Come in, gentlemen, and have a seat." Jimbob and Gemini entered the classroom and took two seats in the front. "Would you care for a spot of tea?"

"No thanks," answered Gemini and Jimbob simultaneously.

"Well, Professor Rabbit, I did lose my mind when I came here, but I found most of it," Gemini said honestly.

Professor Rabbit laughed until he realized that Gemini wasn't joking. "Well, that must have been an adventure. What brings you to the Tooniversity today?"

Jimbob spoke up, "Gemini fainted after–"

"I did not faint!" Gemini shouted at the eggplant. "I blacked out. There's a big difference."

"Fine. Gemini blacked out . . ." he paused and gave Gemini an are-you-happy look. "After battling the shadowy figure that has been attacking residents of Toonopolis."

The rabbit looked up from his pot of tea with more alertness. "I heard about him. He's found a way to kill toons inside the Tooniverse. He has defied all cartoon logic."

"Now there's an oxymoron," quipped Gemini. He looked at Jimbob. "When you said that you couldn't kill cartoons by traditional ways, I assumed that there were nontraditional ways."

Jimbob nodded and agreed, "There is one that I know of: kill the being that created the thought. Do that, and the thought that lives in the Tooniverse is gone."

"And how does a cartoon do that?"

"They can't," answered Professor Rabbit.

Gemini threw his hands in the air. "Then why is it even considered a way if it isn't possible?"

The rabbit took a sip of his tea and shook his finger at the Outsider sitting in his classroom. "Rule number one in cartoon laws: nothing is impossible."

"Then it's been done?"

"Nope," replied Professor Rabbit, "but just because something has not yet been done, does not mean that it can't be done."

Gemini began to object but had to accept the logic of the statement, as twisted as it was. "Well, wouldn't that same law apply to Earth then, also? I mean, what one person says is impossible could always become possible later."

Professor Rabbit clapped his hands together and smiled. He spoke to Jimbob the Talking Eggplant, "What a bright student you've brought me! You are absolutely correct, young man. The difference, however, is that possibilities in the Tooniverse are only limited by imagination. As an Outsider, you can be very dangerous to residents of Toonopolis."

"Why is that?" Gemini asked.

"Creations, like myself, can only operate within the structures of our creator's thoughts of us. We're kind of like computer programs in that way. You, on the other hand, are both present here and still a sentient consciousness at the same time. You can create new thoughts with just your imagination. Therein lies the danger to us all. You could create or . . ." the rabbit left the thought hanging.

Gemini finished the professor's thought, "Or I could destroy." Gemini's eyes flashed with the realization. "Then isn't it likely that Shadowy Figure is an Outsider? No one else has been able to kill toons, but he has found a way. He absorbs them into himself. Could any regular creation do that?"

"Unlikely," Jimbob answered after being quiet for longer than he was accustomed. "So, it might be another Outsider. Let me make a few calls while you get some cartoon physics lessons. Next time you see Shadowy Figure, you need to be prepared so you don't faint—"

"Black out!" Gemini corrected him.

Jimbob smiled at the boy and said, "Black out again." Jimbob bounced out of his chair and bobbed his way out of the classroom leaving Gemini alone with the rabbit in the tweed coat.

"Now," said Professor Rabbit, "let's start with some basic lessons." The professor stood up, walked to his chalkboard, and quickly drew a picture of a cartoon dog that had just walked off the edge of a cliff.

"Gravity does not take effect on a cartoon until said cartoon realizes that gravity should take effect. We call this Gravity Effectiveness Displacement. The trick to exploiting this rule is to remember to never look down while running. If you never know there isn't ground below your feet, you'll never fall off a cliff."

"But wouldn't I have to keep running forever if there isn't ground on the other side of the cliff?"

The rabbit laughed. "In theory, yes, but most of the time cartoons fall eventually. The irony of having the knowledge of this law is that most cartoons still can't resist the urge to look down."

Gemini reached back into his own memories of watching cartoons and couldn't object to the professor's point. He recalled plenty of times when even the protagonist in a cartoon would eventually fall prey to gravity's effects.

"It is important that you don't allow your own curiosity to make you forget that you can control gravity only if you don't think about it. It is a difficult paradox to control but one that can be very helpful to anyone in the Tooniverse, creation or Outsider. Remember," he said, holding a finger in the air, "curiosity killed the cat."

Gemini nodded at Professor Rabbit and absorbed the warning somewhere in his mind. He watched the rabbit teacher walk to a closet at the front of the room. The professor opened the door and retrieved a black and white cat from inside.

"Speaking of cats, here is lesson two: Feline Matter Rearrangement Impermanence, or FMRI."

"Say what?" Gemini responded.

"Anything done to a cat is not permanent. For example, if I were to drop an anvil on the cat," the professor said.

He placed the cat on the ground. The black and white feline looked around nervously. Professor Rabbit retrieved from his desk a remote control with a single red button. When he pressed the button, a cartoon-style anvil fell from the ceiling onto the cat. Gemini gasped at the blatant violence right in front of him.

"Don't worry," the rabbit said, "he's fine."

He pressed the red button again and the anvil flew back into the air. The cat was left as a two-dimensional circle, much like a Frisbee, on the ground. After a few seconds, the cat popped back into its original form.

"You see. No damage done." The cat shot a hateful glare at the professor, suggesting that it did not agree with his analysis of the situation. "Well, permanent damage at least. Thank you, Chairman Meow." He placed the cat back into the closet.

"Lesson three is a very important one, especially for an Outsider such as yourself. This lesson involves the use of C-spaces."

"Cartoon spaces?"

"Good guess, yes. C-spaces are the rifts in cartoon space where cartoons can pull objects seemingly from nowhere. For creation toons, we can only pull out objects related to our creator's vision of us. For example," Professor Rabbit said as he pulled an overhead projector out from behind his back, "I can pull out teaching aids from C-spaces. Basically, anything that serves a purpose for us is accessible. You, on the other hand, could theoretically produce anything you wanted. You'd just have to imagine what you were grabbing and it will appear. Why don't you try it?"

Gemini stood up. He reached behind his back and tried to focus on a metal sword, something that he felt would have been more helpful to him when Shadowy Figure attacked. As he attempted to pull the sword from C-space, the classroom door opened.

When he yanked his hands in front of him, he heard the classroom door open and found that he was holding out his tighty-whitey underwear on display. Jimbob the Talking Eggplant began laughing hysterically as he rolled into the room.

Professor Rabbit shook his head and smiled. "I should have warned you that any lack of focus will invariably result in an embarrassing situation for you. That is not really a cartoon law of physics per se, but it is still a good rule to remember."

Jimbob righted himself and stopped laughing. "Well, thanks for the information, Professor." He turned to Gemini, who was struggling to shove his underwear back into his pants.

"If you're done airing your dirty laundry, we've got a new destination. I called the people over at Sorting Square, and they said that they know of only one other Outsider currently in Toonopolis."

Gemini shook off his embarrassment and peered at his purple mentor. "Who? Where?" he asked.

"His name is Jack Montana, and he runs a fighting league over in the Warehouse Area of Toonopolis."

"Then I guess we should pay him a visit and see if we can get any information out of him," Gemini said. He nodded his thanks to Professor Rabbit, and he and Jimbob left the Tooniversity classroom to set off for the Warehouse Area.

Chapter Five

Warehouse Area

Gemini and Jimbob the Talking Eggplant arrived in the Warehouse Area, and for the first time since his arrival in Toonopolis, Gemini felt like he actually had a sense of purpose. With the majority of his memories restored, he felt much more confident in his ability to face off with Shadowy Figure should he meet the specter again.

The two companions walked down an abandoned road shadowed on both sides by massive nondescript warehouses. The only warehouse that stood out lay at the end of the road on which they were walking. It had a large, brightly colored sign that read "Toonopolis Fighting World" in flashing lights of every neon shade imaginable.

"So," Gemini began, "what do you know about Fighting World?"

"Just what the Sorting Square people told me. Jack Montana came here years ago. Like you, he is an Outsider. He found his way here and started this cartoon fighting league. It's like pro wrestling with a cartoon twist."

Jimbob continued as they arrived at the front of the building, "He's been pretty low-key, as far as they can tell. His Tooniverse guide left him alone a while ago."

"What kind of cartoons are involved with this Fighting World?"

"That's the crazy part. Somehow, Montana has drawn in toons from all over Toonopolis. You'd think it would only appeal to toons that were created for fighting, but there's every manner of cartoon involved, which doesn't really make sense."

Gemini nodded and arched his neck to look at the flashy sign at the top of the warehouse. "Sounds suspicious to me. Professor Rabbit said that creations could only function within their design. If a toon wasn't created for fighting, how could it fight?"

"Well," said Jimbob, "when an Outsider is involved, all cartoon rules can become null and void. Let's ask Jack Montana about that." Jimbob pushed an overly large doorbell next to the warehouse entrance. The doorbell played an elevator-music version of the Mortal Kombat theme song. "Well, that's fitting, I guess."

"Not really," Gemini said. "For cartoons, wouldn't it be considered immortal combat instead?"

"Good point," Jimbob agreed.

A peephole slid open, and a pair of red eyes looked out at Gemini and Jimbob. "What do you want? The next show doesn't start until Saturday morning."

Gemini looked at Jimbob and recalled his guide telling him that it was always Saturday morning in Toonopolis. Jimbob waved him off. "We're here to see Jack Montana," said Jimbob.

"We're not recruiting new fighters right now, so come back another day," said the voice belonging to the eyes. The peephole slid shut quickly, leaving Jimbob and Gemini staring at the warehouse door.

"I get the feeling that we're not welcome," Gemini said to Jimbob. "But I have an idea." Gemini reached behind him and pulled out two fake mustaches and a box wrapped in brown paper. He placed one of the mustaches on his upper lip and handed the second to Jimbob.

Jimbob glared at the mustache and then looked back up at Gemini. "Your plan is to fool them into thinking that we're different people delivering a package?"

"Why not?"

"Well, in case you haven't noticed, I'm a giant eggplant."

"And?"

"I'm not sure that a mustache on a giant eggplant makes much of a difference in identifying said eggplant, even in a cartoon world."

Gemini laughed. "If we're dealing with a toon behind that door, it will work. If a pair of glasses can turn Superman into Clark Kent, then a mustache can turn a two-foot talking eggplant into–"

Jimbob interrupted him, "A two-foot talking eggplant with a mustache!" Jimbob put on the mustache and stroked it in an evil-genius motion.

"It's so crazy it just might work." Jimbob then looked up at Gemini. "On second thought, you're an idiot."

This suggestion caused Gemini to take the box he was carrying and slam it down over Jimbob the Talking Eggplant, sealing him inside. Gemini picked up the box and rang the Mortal Kombat doorbell again.

From within the box, Jimbob called out, "I change my mind. I want to try to the mustache thing."

"Too late," Gemini said. "Maybe next time you'll trust me."

The peephole slid open, and the same red eyes peered down at Gemini, now clad in his foolproof mustache disguise and carrying what was obviously a delivery package. "Package for Jack Montana," Gemini said. He lowered his voice in an attempt to sound old enough to actually be able to grow a mustache. The peephole slid shut, and Gemini could hear the un-clicking of locks.

The door swung open and revealed that the red eyes belonged to a coat rack. The eyes floated a little off the top of the coat rack, and there was a very small mouth on its trunk. "Right this way, sir," said the coat rack, leading Gemini down a hallway. Gemini opened the lid of the box and peered in at Jimbob, who gave a purple thumbs-up from within.

"Right through here," the coat rack said, pointing through a doorway.

"Thanks," said Gemini as he ducked into a darkened room. He walked until he felt the ground change underneath his feet. He found himself standing in something that felt like sand or loose dirt. "Jimbob, this doesn't feel right."

"As it shouldn't," came a voice from above Gemini. A series of bright lights suddenly blinked on, and Gemini found himself standing in the middle of a large pit with bleachers around it. Gemini searched the bleachers for the source of the voice, and his eyes fell on a pale man standing at the edge of the pit. "So, Gemini, we meet again."

Gemini felt an eerie wave shiver down his spine. "So, we have met before, huh?"

"No," said the man, "but it seemed more dramatic if I said it that way."

Gemini glared at the pale man standing in front of him. He appeared to be nearly six feet tall from where Gemini was standing but was rail thin. He had wild black eyes and a receding hairline. He was wearing khaki pants and a white button-down shirt that was partially tucked in.

"Then how did you know my name?"

"Information about an Outsider coming into the Tooniverse travels quickly, and I have my sources," he said, followed by an off-kilter cackle.

"Um, can I get out now?" asked Jimbob from within his cramped quarters. Gemini dropped the box with a start. He had forgotten that his companion was inside. The box broke open and Jimbob tumbled out.

"Oh, a two-foot-tall talking eggplant with a mustache. Now there's a good disguise."

"I tried to tell him it was dumb," said Jimbob as he stood up and shook the pit's dirt off his purple skin. "But who would listen to their Tooniverse guide, am I right, Jack?" He looked at the man standing in the bleachers.

Jack applauded Jimbob's recognition of him. "I guess the cat's out of the bag. Or the eggplant's out of the box might be more appropriate. Why are you here, Gemini? Didn't your guide tell you that it's best for Outsiders to stay away from each other? Our power scares the little toons."

"What are you talking about, Montana?" asked Gemini.

"They give you a guide to keep track of you. They don't want us Outsiders to realize our full potential." His wild eyes grew with anxiety as he spoke. "They want to hold us back and get us back to our own worlds. BUT I AM NOT GOING BACK!

THEY CAN'T MAKE ME! I'M NOT GOING BACK TO THAT EXISTENCE!"

Gemini looked to Jimbob for an explanation. Jimbob merely shrugged and whispered, "Remember how I said most Outsiders didn't stay sane when they crossed over? I'm not sure this guy had a full deck to begin with."

"So they weren't strong enough to get rid of me on their own and now they recruit another Outsider to try to make me leave? Good luck, kid. I've got more power than you think. I'll show them all. I'LL SHOW THEM ALL!"

Throughout his rant, Jack Montana became more and more irritated. His left hand twitched repeatedly, and his head was jerking around. Gemini and Jimbob the Talking Eggplant just stared at him.

"But you walked right into my trap. I heard there was another Outsider in Toonopolis, and I knew they'd send you after me. I'll show you. ATTACK, MY FIGHTERS!"

At his final command, three creatures appeared from previously obscured doorways inside the pit. Jimbob hid behind Gemini as a semicircle of fearsome fighters stood before them. A minotaur stood on the left, wielding a large spiked club over his giant bull head, a ten-foot-tall cyclops with a tree in his hands was in the middle, and on the right was a stuffed teddy bear that was shorter than Jimbob. One of the bear's button eyes dangled from a string halfway down his face.

Gemini eyeballed the creatures in front of him from left to right, his fear growing exponentially at each creature until he reached the teddy bear and laughed. "Seriously, Jack? A teddy bear? That's what you're sending after me?"

In response, the teddy bear pulled a rocket launcher from the C-space behind him and set its sights on Gemini and his purple friend. "Oh," Gemini said, "I see." He stuck his hands behind his back. "Two can play that game!" he shouted as he pulled his hands to the front.

He was holding a purple oval-shaped object with a face. Jimbob waved at Gemini and grimaced. "Um, are you going to throw me at them?"

"Good idea!"

"Noooooo!" cried Jimbob the Talking Eggplant as Gemini hurled him toward the cyclops in the middle of the semicircle. The giant swept Jimbob aside with one large hand and growled.

To his right, the teddy bear let loose a rocket toward Gemini. "Yes," Jack Montana shrieked. "Get him, my champion. Destroy him, Fluffybear!"

Gemini tumbled to the side, narrowly escaping the rocket as it exploded against the side of the pit. He looked up at Jack and asked, "Your champion's name is Fluffybear?"

"Looks can be deceiving, kid. Now I'll leave you to play with my fighters. I've got business to attend to, and I will not have you disrupt my master plan."

From above the pit, a beam of light shone down next to Jack Montana. Riding down the beam to his side was an angel dressed in white leather. The top of her leather suit was unzipped, revealing a little more than a cartoon should. Her hair was golden blond, and she had a sparkling halo floating above her head. Her white-feathered wings gently arched so she could glide gracefully down.

"Excuse me, but my ride is here. Ta-ta!" The angel picked up Jack in her arms and flew the two of them back up the beam of light and out of the fighting pit. Gemini was snapped back into reality by the minotaur's club smacking him into the wall next to a purple splotch that was once Jimbob.

The two of them fell to the ground and regained their proper forms. "I can't believe it," said Jimbob as his eyes looked up toward the sky. "He's teamed up with a Rogue. That's not good."

Gemini started to ask a question about the angel when the thundering footsteps of the two lumbering creatures regained his attention. He once again reached back into C-space and ensured that his toon guide wasn't behind him this time. He pulled out a box labeled "black holes."

"An oldie but a goodie," said Jimbob, nodding in approval.

Gemini took out a large black hole and threw it at the feet of the minotaur, who promptly fell into the hole but got stuck at his shoulders. Jimbob ran over to the minotaur and began jumping on his head, trying send him into the hole.

Gemini tried to grab another hole, but the cyclops kicked him across the fighting pit floor. Fortunately, Gemini crashed into a rocket-reloading stuffed animal named Fluffybear, stopping the huggable maniac from firing a rocket into Gemini's face.

Disoriented, Fluffybear got to his feet and fired another rocket right at the cyclops, whose face was blackened by the explosion. After a moment of trying to get his balance, the cyclops fell backwards with a loud crash, shaking the entire warehouse.

Gemini grabbed the teddy bear by the scruff of his neck and lifted him off the ground. "No more high explosives for you. You're getting a time-out, mister." The bear flung his arms and legs, trying to injure Gemini any way he could. He finally tired and hung limp and dejected in the boy's hand.

Jimbob finished pushing the minotaur into the black hole and hopped to Gemini's side. "Man, you should join this fighting league. I bet you'd win every fight."

Gemini rolled his eyes at Jimbob and tied Fluffybear's arms and legs with a rope he pulled from C-space. He placed the trussed teddy bear on the ground in front of him.

"Now," said Gemini, "what was your employer talking about, his master plan? Does it have anything to do with killing toons?"

Fluffybear spit a wad of fluff at Gemini. "You'll never make me talk, copper. I'm no rat, see."

"Oh great, he talks like a bad 1930s gangster. I really don't like this bear," said Jimbob, who spit a purple wad of eggplant seeds into the bear's good eye.

"Jimbob!" scolded Gemini.

"What? He spit on you. I was just making it even."

"You ain't gonna get nuthin' outta me, Outsider. I work for Jack Montana, and he's gonna change the way things operate around here, see."

Gemini stood up, deciding not to waste his time with an exchange he had seen thousands of times on television. "Well, at least it wasn't a waste of time coming here, Jimbob," he wisecracked.

"Yeah, at least we got exercise?"

"I was being sarcastic."

"I knew that."

Gemini took a deep breath and looked at the chaos of the fighting pit—a knocked out cyclops, a giant black hole, and a tied-up teddy bear. He thought about what Jimbob called the angel that took Jack Montana away from the scene.

"What's a Rogue?" he asked.

Jimbob looked grim. "I don't even like talking about them. They're almost as rare in Toonopolis as Outsiders. There's only one place in Toonopolis to find out about Rogues. We have to go to the Black Light District. If Jack Montana is working with that Rogue, Angel, someone there will have the info."

"Her name is Angel?"

"I told you some creators aren't very imaginative with their names."

"I guess. Well, if we have to get information about Rogues, what are we waiting for?" asked Gemini.

Jimbob sighed. "It's not a good place for kids."

"I'm not a kid. I'm a teenager, a young adult."

"Oh yeah? How often do you shave?"

"Shut up," Gemini retorted.

Jimbob mumbled under his breath, "Nice comeback."

"I heard that! Now show me the way to the Black Light District, guide."

"Fine," conceded Jimbob the Talking Eggplant. The two of them walked out of the fighting pit without giving any more thought to the destruction they left behind.

Chapter Six

Black Light District

Wh**hen Gemini rounded a corner and was faced**
with the Black Light District of Toonopolis,
he understood immediately why Jimbob the Talking
Eggplant said that it was not for children. The
cartoons that populated this district were of the
shadiest sort that might be seen on a cable channel
after ten o'clock at night, when all good little boys
were asleep.

In addition to the unsavory characters walking the streets, Gemini found it hard to focus. All of the lights lining the streets were purple-tinted black lights, throwing everything into a lurid haze and turning anything white iridescent. Fluorescent graffiti covered the buildings and glowed under the black lights.

Gemini turned to look at his purple companion and could barely make him out. If it weren't for the brightly glowing teeth in the eggplant's mouth, Gemini probably wouldn't have been able to see Jimbob at all. "So this is the Black Light District?"

"Figured that out all on your own, eh, kid?" was Jimbob's snappy reply.

"Stop calling me that."

"Okay, young adult," Jimbob said to mock their conversation in the Warehouse Area.

"Better, I guess," Gemini halfheartedly accepted. He pondered his next question before deciding if it was worth asking. "What section of Toonopolis are you from, Jimbob?"

"None, really," the eggplant responded. "When I first got here, they had trouble placing me. I mean, where would you put a talking vegetable?"

"A farm, maybe?"

"Yeah, we tried that. I didn't really feel comfortable there. Not very much conversation to be had once those Veggie Tales guys got TMed."

"Who?"

"Some other talking vegetables. They were kind of annoying. Anyway, I ended up just wandering around Toonopolis and learning all about the different parts. That's why I decided to become a guide not too long ago."

"And then I got stuck with you," Gemini said.

Jimbob nodded, "Yes, then you got . . . Hey!"

Gemini smiled. "I'm just kidding. I'm glad I got stuck with you."

Gemini peered down a few alleyways as they walked and saw silhouetted figures in the darkness. He couldn't make out what was going on down the alleys and was happy for that. He sped up a little bit to get past shadiness faster.

"So I guess this is where the 'bad' cartoons end up?" he asked Jimbob.

"Well, 'bad' is really relative. They're only what their creators make them into. The only 'bad' toons are ones that don't act the way they're supposed to." Jimbob caught up to Gemini, and the two of them walked down the street side by side.

Gemini thought about Angel, the angel he saw at Jack Montana's Fighting World. "Rogues?" he ventured.

"Exactly. Nothing worse than a Rogue. They fight against what their creators envisioned them to be."

"How can a toon do that? The professor at the Tooniversity said that creations were like computer programs."

Jimbob nodded, and Gemini assumed he was frowning because he couldn't see his illuminated teeth in the black light. "Yeah, and Rogues are like viruses, if you want to keep using the computer analogy," he said.

"How is that?"

"The link between creator and creation is supposed to be a one-way street; creator has thoughts, thoughts exist."

Jimbob led Gemini down another street, avoiding a group of scantily clad cartoon females. "Rogues travel the wrong way on the one-way street and force their creators to change their idea of them."

"That doesn't sound so bad," said Gemini. "I'm sure a lot of toons would like to do that."

"No, we don't." Jimbob said without looking at Gemini. "Toons aren't built like that. That's what makes Rogues so grotesque. Creations don't have their own will; they aren't supposed to. And when they take it upon themselves to have one, well, it isn't good for their creators."

"Why is that?"

Jimbob stopped in front of a door painted with fluorescent green, gold, and red stripes that glimmered under the black lights. He looked at Gemini.

"Imagine you have an idea about something." Gemini nodded. "Now imagine that idea comes back into your mind and warps itself into something else." Gemini nodded again. "What would your perception of reality be after that?"

Gemini nodded his head one more time as Jimbob knocked on the colorful door. "I guess I'd be a little messed up."

"To say the least," Jimbob replied. "Most times beings that have been Rogued end up insane." He paused. "Or dead, if they're lucky. Of course, a dead creator equals a dead toon, so most would accept what they are rather than risk nonexistence."

The multicolored door opened up, and Gemini looked over Jimbob's shoulder at the creature that opened the door. He was a three-foot-high brown mole and wore a brightly colored hat with the same pattern as the paint on the outside of the building.

He also had on a vest that matched his hat. Streaming down around his face were thick dreadlocks.

"Eh, mon, whatche be needin'?" asked the dreadlocked mole.

"Rastamole, I'm Jimbob the Talking Eggplant and this is Gemini, an Outsider. I'm not here to shop. I'm here for information."

Rastamole nodded his head. "Either way, it not be matterin' to me. I sell bot'." Rastamole waved his stubby arm to invite Jimbob and Gemini into his store.

Jimbob shook his head. "I'd rather not bring the kid in there, Rastamole, if you don't mind. We're not looking for any information that needs to stay private. I need to ask you about Rogues, namely Angel."

Rastamole's face split into a smile of remembrance. "Yeah, mon, what about dat fine little mama?"

"Well, we just had a run-in with Jack Montana over in the Warehouse Area and she was with him. We also had a run-in with the shadowy figure that's been killing toons. We need to find out if the two are related."

Rastamole looked at Gemini. "You just be a beacon o' good luck, eh, mon?" Gemini grimaced at him. "Well, I dunno if dey be related, but dere's been some heavy Rogue activity lately."

"So Angel's not the only one?" Gemini asked.

"No, mon, I been hearin' 'bout a couple more Rogues appearin' recently. One over in Supercity been causin' some trouble. Animetown and Camenot be havin' problems too."

"I have a hard time believing that all of this is coincidence," Jimbob said. "Thanks for the information, Rastamole." Jimbob reached out his magically appearing purple hand and slid something into Rastamole's hand. Gemini assumed Jimbob had paid the mole for his information.

"Anytime, mon. Anytime."

Gemini and Jimbob walked away from Rastamole's place and thought about the new information they had to add to their own experiences.

Gemini broke the silence, "I thought you said Rogues were rare."

"So are Outsiders and there's two of you right now. But four confirmed Rogues all at the same time? I doubt that's ever happened in the history of Toonopolis. This all has to be connected somehow."

A weasel in an overcoat interrupted their conversation. Standing in front of Gemini and

Jimbob, he opened the left side his coat to reveal an array of different watches lining the inside. "Wanna buy a watch?" asked the weasel.

"No," said Jimbob.

"Genuine fake imports here," he persisted.

"He said no," Gemini replied.

The weasel opened the right side of the coat that was lined with a bunch of different types of eyeballs. "How about an eyeball?" the weasel asked.

"Eew, no." Jimbob shuddered and quickly ushered Gemini away from the shady weasel. "Why would he even have eyeballs?" he muttered to himself. Gemini observed his guide, who looked very disturbed. He could see that Jimbob was continuing to mumble to himself but could not make out what else he was saying.

"So, where to next, Señor Crankypants?" Gemini asked, trying to lighten the mood.

"We need more information on Angel. We need to talk to Madame Rouge."

"Rouge is an expert on Rogues?"

Jimbob nodded. "Yes, and on spelling the two words correctly. More specifically, she's an expert on Angel; she used to work here." Jimbob pointed at a building marked only with red fluorescent lighting.

"What's here?" asked Gemini.

"A building," came Jimbob's short reply.

"So, how is Angel a Rogue? I guess she wasn't always meant to be, erm, dressed like she dresses?" Gemini asked bashfully.

"She was supposed to be a sweet, innocent toon. She decided she wanted to be what she is now and warped her creator's mind. She also used to be the only known Rogue, and respectable toons stayed away from her."

Gemini shook his head as Jimbob knocked on the red-tinged door. It opened, and a humanoid red fox was standing in the entranceway. Madame Rouge was wearing a red silk robe and had long red hair that was a slightly brighter shade than her red fur. "You guys cops?" asked the fox.

"Do we look like cops?" asked Gemini.

Madame Rouge gazed at the young man and his giant eggplant partner. "In the Tooniverse . . ."

"Yeah, I know, I know," conceded Gemini. "No, we aren't cops. We're just here to ask you about Angel and what you know of her connection with Jack Montana."

Rouge made a sour face. "That Outsider," she spat out. "Came here talking to my best employee about how he was going to change Toonopolis forever. Got her all riled up and excited. Not that it's too hard to get her excited."

"Do you know what his plan was?" Gemini asked.

"No," she said. "He didn't share it with me. He was specifically looking for Angel."

"Because she's a Rogue?" asked Jimbob the Talking Eggplant.

"Maybe. I don't know for sure. All I know is that he came here, talked to her, and she left with him."

"Rastamole told us there's been more Rogues appearing in other sections of Toonopolis. Have you heard about that?" Jimbob asked.

Madame Rouge sighed. "Rogues, Outsiders, that shadowy guy. Getting hard for an honest woman to make a living in Toonopolis anymore."

When Rouge mentioned Shadowy Figure's name, Gemini felt a cold shiver run down his back. "Shadowy Figure's been here?" he asked nervously.

"Is that his name?" she asked. Gemini nodded. "Okay, I guess. He was here a while ago. Creepy guy."

Jimbob interjected with a question. "Did he hurt anyone? Did he kill any toons in the Black Light District?"

"He can kill toons?" Rouge asked in shock.

Gemini answered, "Yes, he has been absorbing toons and killing them."

Madame Rouge shuddered. "To think he was here. I didn't realize he was that bad. He seemed a little out of it, like he was confused and disoriented. He had a conversation with Angel and then left the Black Light District."

Jimbob nodded. "Thanks, Madame Rouge."

"Any time, cutie," said the red fox as she closed the door.

Jimbob sat down on the steps leading to Madame Rouge's door. "So, Shadowy Figure talks to Angel, and we have new Rogues popping up all over Toonopolis. Jack Montana recruits Angel to 'change Toonopolis forever.'"

"All I know is that I need to find Shadowy Figure and see if I can get the rest of my memories back."

"And find out how to get home," added Jimbob.

"Eh, maybe," responded Gemini.

Jimbob looked a little surprised. "You don't want to go back?"

"What am I going back to? I've got no friends on Earth. My mom left us because my dad was too focused on his research, and my dad used me as a test subject for his experiment and then abandoned me in the Tooniverse. At least here I can be someone."

"You don't know that your dad's abandoned you. Maybe he's trying to figure out a way to get you back right now!"

Gemini scoffed at him. "Unlikely. His research is more important to him than his family."

There was a moment of silence as Jimbob absorbed all that Gemini had just spilled out before him. Gemini looked down at the ground and stared at the dark space between his glowing white shoes.

"But to be someone," said Gemini, "I need to take care of Shadowy Figure and these Rogues. Where did Rastamole say there were new Rogues?"

"Supercity, Animetown, and Camenot," Jimbob supplied.

"Well let's go talk to these Rogues and figure out what's going on. Maybe they can lead us to more information about Jack Montana's plan and finding out what Shadowy Figure's ultimate goal is."

"I still can't believe you don't want to go back to Earth."

"Even if I wanted to, we don't know how, and as you said when we first met, who knows what would happen to an incomplete Outsider who travels back to Earth."

Jimbob nodded in reluctant agreement.

"Maybe we should focus on getting my memory back before we even worry about whether or not I will go home." Gemini felt that he had already made up his mind about whether or not to return to Earth. Jimbob didn't seem to want to accept that decision so he kept it to himself.

"Then," Jimbob said, "let's go visit Supercity and find out what kind of Rogue we'll see there."

The two companions stood up and walked down the dark Black Light District street. They admired the myriad graffiti drawn with the fluorescent paint that lifted off the walls in a 3D effect. They also avoided making eye contact with any of the unsavory characters that populated the district.

Agent Log: Project Gemini
Entry Number: 8
Date: June 3

It seems that my confidence of a few weeks ago was a little premature. After the incident where Jacob Grenk's brain-wave activity spiked, there was an immediate drop-off in confirmed hits from the list we provided the operative during his training.

Doctors Grenk and Kraft were unable to confirm whether there was permanent damage to Jacob's brain that rendered him no longer useful, and I asked them if we should prepare a new subject to continue our work. Dr. Grenk responded a little too quickly that he thought it was a good idea. Dr. Kraft more levelheadedly explained that the subject was seemingly unharmed and it would set us back too far to start over at this juncture.

While I may have been wrong about how perfectly we began this project, it does not seem that I was wrong about Dr. Grenk's emotions becoming too much for him. He has become even more detached than I previously reported. Dr. Kraft told me that a few days ago he observed Dr. Grenk sitting in a chair, staring at a wall for a few hours and mumbling to himself. Once again, I will need to keep a close eye on Grenk while shifting more responsibility to Kraft.

On an interesting note, the targets successfully incapacitated by our Toonopolis operative have been diagnosed with a heretofore unknown psychological disorder. The doctors examining them have called their condition Imagination Deficit Disorder.

The disorder presents as a sudden change in personality, causing the patient to revert to purely animalistic behavior. One researcher cleverly quoted Ayn Rand, saying that the patient was unable to see "beyond the range of the moment." They don't think and barely speak. They are no better than beasts. There are no physical symptoms in the brain visible via MRI Scan. Several papers are being written by famous neurologists on this new phenomenon.

I can't help but laugh, knowing that enemies of the Agency are becoming research fodder while in four-point restraints and drooling on themselves in an insane asylum. I just hope our Tooniverse operative can get back on track soon.

Special Agent Mimic
June 3

Chapter Seven

Supercity

After leaving the seedy underbelly of the Black Light District, Gemini and Jimbob the Talking Eggplant soon found themselves in a new section of Toonopolis, and Gemini noted that Supercity looked drastically different from the sections of Toonopolis that he had previously visited. He hadn't noticed the slight differences in the artistic style before now.

Supercity looked like the drawings in a comic book. All the building lines were very sharp and outlined in black. It also seemed to him if he focused on one building or one vehicle in the street, that it would become more brightly colored while the scenery in the background became duller. He asked Jimbob about this.

"Different places have different styles, of course," Jimbob answered.

Gemini looked at himself and felt that he had not changed at all. "Why don't you and I change too?"

"Because we aren't creations that belong in Supercity. The thoughts that live here were designed to live here, so they look like they belong. Being an Outsider, though, you could change the way you look if you wanted."

Gemini thought about it as they walked. He was so focused that he didn't realize he was about to walk into a streetlamp. The word SMACK literally rose up in the air in front of him. He stared at it while rubbing his forehead.

"Shouldn't it just be the sound that I heard? Why do I see the word?"

Jimbob shrugged what would be his shoulders, if he had any, and answered, "That's comic books for you." Gemini sighed. "But don't worry about that right now. We're here."

Gemini and Jimbob stood at the base of a large skyscraper in Supercity. Large bold lettering down the side of the building spelled out "League Of Superheroes Exuding Righteousness." Gemini looked down at his purple friend and sighed once again.

"Something wrong?" asked Jimbob with a knowing grin.

"Are they aware that their name is an acronym for LOSER? Or are they just that stupid?" Gemini held up a hand to stop Jimbob from responding to the rhetorical question. "Let's just go find out about this Supercity Rogue and see if we can't get some information about Shadowy Figure."

Jimbob nodded and the two of them walked through the skyscraper's revolving doors. Gemini found himself in a large room with marble floors and tall columns on either side. Across from the doorway sat a regular-looking doorman reading a newspaper. He took a few steps toward the doorman before realizing that Jimbob was not with him.

"Wheeeee!" he heard from behind him. He winced in concern for what he would see when he turned around. He watched Jimbob twirling in the revolving door rapidly. The eggplant was spinning so fast that Gemini could only see a purple stripe cutting through the air.

The stripe vanished as Jimbob flew out of the door and thudded into the doorman's desk.

Gemini ran to help his Tooniverse guide get to his feet. The doorman put down his newspaper and peered over the desk at the boy and the vegetable on the floor.

"Can I help you gentlemen?" he asked.

Gemini propped Jimbob up and answered, "We want to speak with the League of Super-righteous-eggs." Gemini wasn't sure he got the name right but also didn't care very much.

The doorman narrowed his eyes at Gemini. "I'm not sure what you're talking about. This is just an office building. There are no superheroes here."

"There's a giant sign on the outside of the building!" Gemini snapped. "Don't tell me this is some secret sanctum when there are fifty feet of lettering identifying this building as the home of the LOSERs."

The doorman looked stunned. He just stared at Gemini without saying a word.

"I think you broke him," suggested Jimbob the Talking Eggplant.

"Whatever," grumbled Gemini, who walked around the desk and began looking around under the doorman's desktop.

"What are you doing?" asked the befuddled doorman.

"Looking for the secret switch that opens a secret door or activates the unrealistically designed platform elevator on the floor."

The doorman looked at Jimbob. "How does he know all of this?"

"Outsider," was all the eggplant had to say in response. The doorman shook his head in acknowledgment as a clicking sound was heard.

"Found it," Gemini said as he came out from under the desk. "Let's go stand on that giant *L* on the floor." Gemini ignored the doorman's pleas and led Jimbob to the center of the floor. After a few seconds, a rope ladder fell from the ceiling, and the end landed on the floor in front of Gemini and Jimbob. The two of them stared blankly for a moment at the ladder.

Jimbob laughed. "What is this? A tree fort?"

"So much for a high-tech and super cool underground fortress," Gemini said as he placed a foot on the rope ladder. He began climbing. "If I get up there and they're in sleeping bags making s'mores, I'm going to be very upset."

He reached the top of the ladder, peered over the edge, and was somewhat surprised to find that the League Of Superheroes Exuding Righteousness did not, in fact, hang out in a tree fort. He emerged in the corner of a large, open room with a circular table in the center. A group that he figured were the superheroes was sitting around the table and engaged in a heated discussion.

"How would you feel if it were your sidekick, Miss Fire?" asked a muscular man wearing red, white, and blue spandex. He was talking to a red-headed woman wearing a red and orange jumpsuit and an orange cape decorated in flames.

"Look, Lord Liberty, it isn't my sidekick we're talking about here. It's yours. That puts a heavier part of the blame on your shoulders. If you had raised him properly, maybe this wouldn't have happened."

Jimbob the Talking Eggplant popped his head above the rope ladder hole and observed the scene also. Gemini looked at him and whispered, "They're talking about sidekicks like they're children."

"Aren't they?" asked Jimbob.

Gemini noticed a third being sitting at the table, but he remained seated and quiet. He looked like a large humanoid brown bear. He stood up and must have towered over seven feet tall. He wore nothing but a yellow pair of Speedo-style shorts. He pounded a huge fist on the circular table.

"We will solve nothing by fighting with one another. The blame falls solely on Plucky. He chose to go Rogue. It is not Lord Liberty's fault.

It is no one's fault except that villainous shadow man who showed up and encouraged him to do it."

The bear-man spoke with a sense of calm that belied his shaggy, fierce exterior. Miss Fire and Lord Liberty looked at each other. Gemini cleared his throat, causing all three members of the League Of Superheroes Exuding Righteousness to look his way.

"How did you get in here?" asked Miss Fire.

"We found the secret switch of predictability and climbed the rope ladder of awesomeness into your lair of . . ." Jimbob began and struggled fore an appropriate adjective to describe an open room with nothing but a circular table in the center. "Cool?" he ventured.

Gemini did not wait for a response to Jimbob's sarcasm. "We came here because the people at Sorting Square said that you were the ones to talk to about a Rogue in Supercity. I am Gemini, an Outsider to Toonopolis, and I'm on a journey to defeat Shadowy Figure. I need to talk to the new Rogues to find out more information."

Lord Liberty approached Gemini as he climbed out of the entranceway and onto his feet. The superhero extended a blue-gloved hand in welcome. "I am Lord Liberty, the young lady there is Miss Fire, and the hairy one is Ursidae. We are members of the League Of Superheroes Exuding Righteousness."

"Yeah, about that name," Gemini said. Lord Liberty looked at him, clearly oblivious to the acronymic implications of their name choice. "Never mind. Who is Plucky?"

"Plucky McGee," Lord Liberty said with a tone of remorse in his voice. "He's been my sidekick for years. A great kid. Always there for me when I needed somebody else to get blown up by something." Liberty paused and grinned until Miss Fire glared at him. "I don't know why he went Rogue."

"Maybe because being a sidekick to a superhero is one of the worst jobs you could possibly have?" suggested Jimbob.

Miss Fire took objection. "Our sidekicks love their jobs! How could you suggest that?"

"Oh yeah? Where are they now?" asked Jimbob suspiciously.

Ursidae responded. "They are where they always go when we have our meetings."

He waved a large bear claw to the right. Gemini and Jimbob followed the claw with their eyes and saw a smaller circular table off to the side of the room. A teenage boy wearing a bear mask and a twenty-something girl with a costume that mirrored Miss Fire's, with the red and orange coloring inverted, sat at the table.

Jimbob started laughing. The three superheroes looked at him puzzlingly. "You put them at the little kids' table?" he managed to spit out between laughs. Gemini smiled.

Miss Fire looked annoyed and spoke up. "Blaze and Little Dipper are not relevant to this discussion. It is *his* sidekick we are worried about," she said, pointing a finger at Lord Liberty.

"I agree," said Gemini, nudging Jimbob with his foot. The eggplant stifled his laughter, but still snorted a muffled guffaw as he tried to get it under control.

"What is your concern regarding the shadow man?" asked Ursidae. Gemini explained to the superheroes his last interaction with Shadowy Figure: the blackout, the recovered memories, and the trail that kept leading Gemini toward him.

"Well," said Lord liberty, "it seems our goal is the same then. You want to find this Shadowy Figure, as you have named him, and I want my Plucky back. My laundry is getting backed up." Miss Fire glared daggers at him. "Okay, fine. I also miss the little guy."

"So what has he done to go Rogue?" Gemini asked.

"The worst thing a sidekick can do," Lord Liberty answered. "He's gone villain."

Ursidae and Miss Fire shook their heads sadly. They each snuck a glance at their sidekicks, clearly thankful that it wasn't one of them that went Rogue.

Liberty continued, "He's gathered up some of our worst enemies and is leading them."

"He's changed his name too," Ursidae added. "He calls himself Midnight now."

Lord Liberty shook his head sadly in the same way his two partners had a moment earlier.

"Well then, shall we go talk to this Midnight? What abandoned warehouse is he hiding in?" Gemini asked.

Lord Liberty looked surprised, letting Gemini know that he had guessed correctly at Midnight's location. Regardless, the superheroes all nodded and began moving toward the exit.

Jimbob looked over at the two sidekicks at the little kids' table. "Should we let the kiddies out of time-out to come play with us?"

Ursidae and Miss Fire looked at each other with some worry. Ursidae answered, "We think it's best not to expose them to Plucky right now."

"Afraid they might be contaminated?" asked Jimbob with a smirk. "I don't think turning Rogue is a disease. It's a mindset."

"Either way," said Miss Fire, "we'd prefer if they stayed here. We need someone to look after our Lair of Cool, as you called it."

The superheroes, Gemini, and Jimbob the Talking Eggplant left the Lair of Cool and headed to another section of Supercity. Leaving behind Blaze and Little Dipper, the five of them set out to bring to justice the former sidekick turned villain.

Their destination turned out to be not too far from the skyscrapers of downtown Supercity. A row of warehouses lined a street that clearly did not receive very much foot traffic. One of the warehouses was the color of darkness. It had obviously been recently painted pitch black. The other warehouses had various colors and symbols on them, suggesting that the row of "abandoned" storage facilities probably saw more use in Supercity than would a similar place on Earth.

"Not very subtle, is he?" Gemini said to Lord Liberty.

"I think he's enjoying being openly defiant, and we can't let that stand. Former sidekick or not, I must live up to my vow of protecting Supercity from all sources of evil. If I must take down Plucky to adhere to that vow, then so be it!"

Jimbob looked at Lord Liberty. "Been practicing that one?"

"A little bit," Lord Liberty admitted.

"Good speech," Miss Fire said. "But it isn't Plucky we're facing; it's Midnight. You need to remember that when the time comes."

Ursidae agreed. "We also need to remember that he's a Rogue now. Who knows what new powers he might have given himself. We're walking into the complete unknown here."

Gemini reached behind his back into C-space and came out wielding a giant mallet that he swung with ease. His eyes narrowed at the superheroes. "Are we ready?"

The superheroes all assumed fighting stances, while Gemini walked to the door and swung the mallet at it, crushing the wooden door open with a loud crash. As the dust and debris settled, Lord Liberty, Miss Fire, and Ursidae ran into the building. Gemini and Jimbob followed.

Gemini expected to jump headlong into a fray with Midnight's minions but was thoroughly surprised to find that the superheroes were not attacked when they entered the building.

"There should be at least ten minions attacking us by now," said a confused Gemini.

"Yeah," the LOSERs all agreed.

Supercity

"What's that?" asked Jimbob the Talking Eggplant, pointing to the end of the warehouse. Sitting on a raised platform was a teenage boy wearing all black with small sparkling white dots decorating his costume. He had on a black eye-mask, similarly speckled. He did not look healthy, and his body slumped in the chair.

"Plucky," whispered Lord Liberty, who began walking slowly toward the young man on the platform.

Gemini's eyes perked up. "It's got to be a trap, Lord Liberty. Be careful!"

"Thanks, Admiral Ackbar," mumbled Jimbob.

Lord Liberty paused, agreeing that Gemini was probably correct. Gemini assumed the new villain was trying to play to his former boss's sympathies.

After a few moments of silence, however, Gemini wasn't so sure he was correct. He began walking toward the platform himself, his mallet raised in anticipation.

"It's no trap," coughed the boy in black. "I'm dying, and my minions have abandoned me. My reign of evil is over before it even started."

Gemini was still leery, but Lord Liberty disregarded his caution and ran to be at his former partner's side. He lifted a black sparkling hand and looked forlorn.

"What's happening, Plucky?"

"Midnight," he corrected between coughs.

"Fine, Midnight, whatever. Why are you dying?"

Midnight smiled a wry smile. "My creator is dying. I guess I pushed him too far. I just didn't want to be a sidekick anymore. I was sick of sitting at the kids' table."

Jimbob pointed at the superheroes accusingly, suggesting he was right in his assertions at the Lair of Cool.

"I was sick of being kidnapped and having to be rescued," Midnight continued. "I was sick of having to wear colors that complimented you, Lord Liberty. I really don't look good in red. And I was sick of having to repeat the same bad puns over and over again."

"I thought you liked your puns," Lord Liberty ventured.

"Oh? 'Looks like that was a close shave, Lord Liberty,' I said after fighting the Mad Barber. When we battled the Trashman: 'I guess we cleaned up this one.' Who would actually enjoy saying things like that?"

Gemini shot a glance at Jimbob, who was wearing a grin and pointing to himself with one of his purple hands. Noticing Gemini's look, Jimbob quickly dropped his grin and assumed a more concerned expression.

A tear came to Lord Liberty's eye as Midnight expressed his lack of satisfaction with his designed sidekick role, and Miss Fire looked like she was ready to cry as well. Ursidae stood his ground with no tears but was clearly touched by Midnight's final words.

Gemini looked at his wrist, pretending to check the time. "Yeah, yeah," he said, "you hated being a sidekick. But that's what you were created to be. You deserve your fate, Rogue. Where is Shadowy Figure?"

The superheroes gasped at Gemini's lack of sympathy for the dying villain, whom they all fondly remembered as Plucky McGee.

Midnight just scoffed. "That lying jerk? He told me it would be okay, that I would be able to get what I wanted. He taught me how to follow the string of consciousness back to my creator. He said he was here to change the way things worked in Toonopolis. I shouldn't have believed him."

Midnight coughed and sputtered. Lord Liberty held him to his chest. "Save your words, young ward. Maybe you can pull through," he said, ever optimistic.

"I don't have long, Lord Liberty. I am sorry. I just wanted to be in charge for once. I wanted to be the boss. I miss being your sidekick. I wish I never met that shadow jerk. I love you, Lord Liberty. And I'm sorry."

With his final words said, Plucky "Midnight" McGee let his head slump down onto his chest. Lord Liberty sobbed as he lifted his friend and former sidekick out of his chair, cradled him in his arms, and walked through the warehouse holding him like a sleeping child. Miss Fire and Ursidae followed solemnly behind.

"Well," Gemini said, "a little dramatic, don't you think? I thought Rogues were supposed to be hated by everyone. And it's just a cartoon after all."

Jimbob dabbed a purple tear from his eye and glared at Gemini. "He may be just a cartoon to you, kid, but he's as real to Lord Liberty as any human you knew on Earth might be to you. Also, don't forget that he was linked to a human on Earth who died with him." Jimbob followed behind the LOSERs to exit the warehouse.

Gemini sat down and felt ashamed at his indifference to Plucky's death. He was starting to realize that this world was very real, and what happened here both affected and was affected by things happening on Earth. He also felt annoyed that he learned nothing about Shadowy Figure from the now-deceased Rogue. With these conflicting feelings, he decided it was best that he leave Supercity behind and head to Animetown, the next known location of one of the new Rogues.

Chapter Eight

Animetown

The journey from Supercity to Animetown was a somber one for Gemini and Jimbob the Talking Eggplant. The death of the Rogue in Supercity left them with no answers and heavy hearts. Gemini also carried the added guilt of his indifference toward the death of the cartoon. The two of them stood outside the entrance to Animetown. Gemini wasn't even sure how they got there since he didn't pay attention to where Jimbob was leading him.

"Wait up!" cried a familiar female voice behind them. They turned to see Miss Fire from Supercity standing with her hand on her hip, trying to catch her breath.

"Miss Fire!" Gemini yelled. "What's wrong? Is everything okay?"

"Fine," she managed to get out between deep breaths. She paused a moment and continued, a little less winded. "You two left without saying goodbye."

"Oh, sorry, goodbye," said Jimbob with a wave.

Miss Fire rolled her eyes. "I wasn't chasing you for a goodbye. I want to come with you on your journey."

Jimbob's eyes went up at that remark. "Are you sure?" he asked.

"After seeing the damage that Shadowy Figure caused in Supercity, I want to help take him down, no matter where he ends up in Toonopolis." She decreed her purpose with such aplomb that Gemini smiled.

"What about Blaze?" Gemini asked.

"She has agreed to sidekick for Lord Liberty. He is still reeling from Plucky's death, but I think Blaze might help him. At least she can be there for him as he recovers."

"Miss Fire, I wanted to apologize—"

The superheroine cut off Gemini, "You don't need to apologize, Gemini. I know you're an Outsider. I know it may be hard for you to accept us creations as 'real.'"

Gemini nodded. "But I do. I was wrong and let my righteousness take over my feelings. I'm sorry."

Miss Fire smiled and placed a hand on Gemini's shoulder. "You're forgiven. I speak for me and for my compatriots in Supercity."

"Well then," Gemini said with a renewed smile, "shall we?"

They turned their attention back to the rustic Japanese village in front of them. The buildings looked vastly different from anything they had seen in Toonopolis thus far. After the tall, sharp-lined buildings in Supercity, the colorful one-story buildings with their slightly upturned roofs seemed even more pleasant. A soft light shone from several of the buildings through the sliding rice paper doors that covered the entranceways.

Miss Fire whistled. "I've never been anywhere in Toonopolis except Sorting Square and Supercity. This place is strange-looking."

Gemini smiled and said, "If I remember Japanese cartoons correctly, we haven't even begun to see strange yet."

Animetown

As if on cue, a group of schoolgirls walked past the trio in a tight cluster, chattering to one another in Japanese. A pair of schoolboys followed a distance behind them. All of them were headed toward a schoolhouse at the end of the paved street.

One of the schoolgirls looked at the odd trio that clearly didn't belong in Animetown and her eyes grew abnormally wide. "KAWAII!" she screamed as she ran toward them. At her high-pitched scream, Gemini, Miss Fire, and Jimbob all covered their ears. When the schoolgirl reached the group, she bent over in front of Jimbob the Talking Eggplant and poked him in the head with a finger.

"What in Toonopolis?" Jimbob responded.

"She thinks you're cute," explained Gemini.

The schoolboys that were following the crowd of girls looked over at the scene and got a good view of the schoolgirl's underpants beneath her skirt as she bent over. They immediately developed nosebleeds, and their jaws dropped open.

Gemini turned to Miss Fire and held out his hand as if to display the scene appearing in front of them. "I told you it would get stranger," he said.

Jimbob looked both confused and scared as the young girl continued to poke and prod him. "Um, Miss? Can you stop doing that please?" She stopped, looking a little surprised that the eggplant spoke.

Gemini waved to get her attention. "Do you know where the Rogue is?" The girl opened her eyes wide and simply blinked at him.

"WHERE IS ROGUE?" Jimbob asked more loudly.

Miss Fire shook her head. "Clearly the young lady doesn't speak English. I don't think repeating the question louder will change that."

"Hang on," said Gemini with an idea. He reached into C-space and pulled out a small black machine with a red button on it. The button was a dial that had three options: Japanese, English Subtitles, and English Dub. It was currently set to Japanese.

"What is that?" asked Miss Fire.

"It's a machine I just made up. It will translate for us. Let's try subtitles," Gemini said. He turned the red dial to English Subtitles.

The girl turned back to the boys who were still staring wide-eyed and bloody-nosed at the schoolgirl. "Danseito no hentai!" she screamed in her glass-breaking wail. Above her head, the words were translated to "Schoolboy pervert!" in a white block script. Her head grew large as she became enraged at the boys, who immediately ran away from her.

"Nah," said Gemini. "I hate subtitles." He turned the red dial to English Dub. The girl's head shrunk back to normal size and she returned to doting upon Jimbob.

"So cute!" they heard the schoolgirl say to Jimbob. It took Gemini a second to realize that she was the one who spoke because her lips did not move in sync with the words. Miss Fire raised a finger as though she wanted to ask about the poor dubbing. Gemini just waved her off.

"Do you know about the Rogue here?" Gemini asked again with the aid of his machine. The schoolgirl froze in fear, and Gemini knew he had a lead. He also became aware that Rogues were not very hard to find.

The schoolgirl nodded. "Anchihiiroo."

"The dubbing thing isn't working," Jimbob said to Gemini. "I have no idea what she just said."

Miss Fire shook her head at the eggplant. "I'm pretty sure that's just the Rogue's name, Jimbob."

The schoolgirl nodded again. A bell rang in the distance, and the girl noticed that her friends had all left her while she admired the two-foot-tall eggplant. "I'm late for school! Ask Yuki if you want more information about Anchihiiroo."

She turned and ran away. Gemini shouted after her, "But who is Yuki?" Gemini wrinkled his brow in consternation, causing a large blue teardrop of sweat to appear on his head.

"What in Toonopolis?" asked Jimbob the Talking Eggplant as he looked at the sweat drop on Gemini's head.

Gemini smiled. "Well, I figured if I'm in Animetown I should follow local customs and accent my emotions with physical effects."

"Well, don't," Jimbob said. "It's creepy."

"Wait until I get angry and I make my head grow two sizes and my body shrink like that girl just did," laughed Gemini.

"Not to spoil the fun," interjected Miss Fire, "but if your little machine translated the Japanese to English, how did she understand us speaking in English to her?"

Gemini looked at Miss Fire and shrugged. "Plot hole?"

"Okay then," she said without enthusiasm. "Maybe we should just try to find this Yuki person. I don't feel comfortable in this place." She looked down at her costume. "I don't really fit in here."

"Okay, Captain Killjoy," muttered Jimbob.

They didn't really know who they were supposed to be looking for, so they decided to walk down the paved road. They opted to follow the path the schoolchildren took earlier toward their school. After a few moments of walking, a large white dog appeared in front of them, looking quizzical by tilting its large head slightly sideways.

Jimbob took a step back in fear. The dog barked at them, but its bark sounded hollow and metallic. Jimbob fell over in a cloud of dust. When he arose, he was wearing a bandage on his head.

"Where did that bandage come from?" asked Gemini.

"What bandage?" Jimbob raised one of his conveniently appearing purple hands to his head and felt a bandage. "I have no idea."

"If you want information on Anchihiiroo, follow me," came a voice from inside the dog. The trio was a little shocked but still followed the white dog when it turned and walked toward a building. There was a sign outside the building with a picture of a crossed wrench and a screwdriver.

Outside the building, Gemini took a closer look at the dog. At first glance, it looked like a real dog, but now that he was closer, he could tell that the dog was made out of metal. It had white hairs secured throughout its body, but its joints were clearly bolted together and its tail made a mechanical whirring sound when it wagged.

The door to the building opened, and a pale man stood at the entranceway. The dog trotted inside the building, and the man smiled at the three visitors to Animetown. He had pale skin, white hair, pink eyes, and he was wearing a white jumpsuit.

"Welcome," said the man. "I'm glad you followed Wan-Wan to my shop. I was worried you wouldn't find me."

"Seriously?" asked Jimbob. "The dog led us about ten feet. Couldn't you have just opened the door and called for us to come over? I mean, that would have been easier then sending out a dog to get our attention."

"But not as much fun," the pale man said. He motioned for them to follow him into the building. Inside, Gemini saw bits of metal, screws, and machinery spread around the place in no real order. It was metallic chaos.

"Who are you?" asked Miss Fire.

"I am Yuki. I am an inventor, and Wan-Wan is my proudest creation." Yuki patted the large white dog on the head with a hollow thumping sound.

The three travellers introduced themselves. Jimbob looked at the dog, impressed. "That dog is a robot? Neat!"

"I prefer to call him a canindroid," Yuki corrected. "I always wanted an Akita but I'm allergic to dog hair."

"Why are you so white?" asked Gemini, bluntly changing the subject. Miss Fire looked at him in dismay. She clearly thought his question was too forward.

"I am an albino. I was born with no skin pigment. No issue really, but that's why my parents named me Yuki, which means 'snow.' But I thought you were here to find out about Anchihiiroo?"

Jimbob cleared a space off one of the counters and sat down. "Yes, we are. What can you tell us about him?"

"First," Yuki began, "he doesn't answer to that name anymore. He calls himself Han'Eiyuu now. He was once one of the most famous heroes in all of Animetown."

Miss Fire sat down next to Jimbob. "But that doesn't make sense. The last Rogue we met was just a sidekick. If he was already a famous hero, why would he go Rogue?"

"Han'Eiyuu became a hero by circumstance, not choice," the albino explained. His voice grew sadder as he began explaining the conditions of the Rogue's upbringing. "He had a terrible childhood. He was orphaned at an early age when his parents were killed in a war. Then his orphanage burned down, and then a flood wiped out the town his orphanage was in. He was the only survivor."

At each additional level of tragedy, Gemini's eyes widened further until they nearly covered his entire face. He shook off the physical effects of the emotion. "How did he become a hero?"

"He trained as a warrior with some of the best martial arts senseis in Animetown and tracked down the ones responsible for killing his parents and burning down the orphanage. He defeated them. Along the way, the townspeople fell in love with him, even though he was always a jerk."

"Why would they train him if he was a jerk?" asked Jimbob. "I mean, I'm a jerk and no one trains me." Miss Fire and Gemini nodded in agreement. Jimbob smiled and then quickly frowned.

Yuki simply shrugged. "Destiny, maybe? Some of them may have felt sympathy for his plight, and some senseis will train anyone with talent, regardless of personality, in the hopes that they will become great students."

"So, what now?" asked Miss Fire.

"He's turned into a villain now. He has begun attacking the townspeople for no reason, and he seems to take satisfaction in their torment. He says he is just following the logical progression to act like a character who has been through as much pain as he has, instead of the unrealistic antihero figure his creator forced him to become."

The three newcomers to Animetown were quiet for a moment while they allowed all the information about the new Rogue to soak in. Gemini felt like he could relate to the abandonment that Han'Eiyuu must have been feeling. He once again thought about how he was stuck in the Tooniverse only for his father's research.

"Why would we be told to talk to you to find out information?" Jimbob asked, breaking the silence.

Yuki took a deep breath and exhaled. "Because he is my brother."

Miss Fire gasped and fell over, seemingly for no reason. She quickly stood back up, a bandage on her head. She ripped it off angrily and threw it to the ground.

"Was it that shocking, Miss?" asked Yuki.

"No, I tripped over a hammer," she said, annoyed. Miss Fire bent down and lifted a hammer from the floor to prove her point. "You need a maid."

"Or a sidekick," Jimbob added with a wink at Miss Fire. The superheroine groaned and flung the hammer at Jimbob, who fell behind a workbench to avoid the projectile.

"Wait," said Gemini, ignoring Miss Fire and Jimbob and attempting to get back on topic. "I thought you said Han'Eiyuu was an orphan and no one from the town survived the flood."

Yuki took a deep breath and prepared to explain, but Jimbob the Talking Eggplant, back upright after his fall, stopped him before he could start. "I think we have had quite enough exposition for today, thank you." He looked at Gemini. "Can't we just accept that they're brothers and not hear the story about how?"

"I agree," Miss Fire said.

Gemini conceded the fact and said to Yuki, "Could you just tell us where to find him?"

The albino inventor looked disappointed at not being allowed to tell his story but seemed to accept it reluctantly. "My brother has taken over the Buddhist temple on the opposite side of town. He is using it as the base for his reign of terror."

"Then let's go have a talk with him," suggested Gemini. "Maybe he'll give us more information than the last Rogue we dealt with."

The group all agreed and filed out of the inventor's shop. Gemini led, followed by Jimbob, Miss Fire, Yuki, and Wan-Wan. As they walked down the path toward the temple occupied by Han'Eiyuu, a light rain began to fall.

"Funny," observed Jimbob, "it was just a clear sky. It seems like the rain only appeared suddenly for some sort of dramatic effect, setting up a more interesting fight sequence."

"Yeah," said Gemini as he tramped through the water that was beginning to pool on the pavement. "I'm beginning to get annoyed at the predictability of Toonopolis." He looked at Miss Fire, who seemed distracted by her hands. "What's wrong?"

"The rain." She frowned. "I am no good to you with my hands wet. I can't ignite my powers in the rain."

The group stopped at the entrance to the temple, a traditional pagoda, five stories tall with winged eaves at each level. A long needle point cut a vertical line in the sky from the highest roof of the temple. They all simultaneously found their gazes resting on a silhouetted figure standing on top of the temple's uppermost roof and holding onto the needle for support.

A flash of lightning lit up the sky, revealing for a brief moment a shirtless figure holding a long curved sword over his shoulder, his long black hair whipping around his body dramatically. He was wearing a pair of black samurai pants and nothing else.

"It is no matter that she cannot help you!" cried the figure atop the temple. He leapt down to the ground in front of Gemini. He towered over Gemini by at least a foot. "If you want to fight me, Gemini, it will be in single combat."

"How do you know me?" Gemini asked over the sound of the rain and the thunder.

"I have been warned that you would be coming for me. You will not take away my freedom and force me to live as a tormented hero again." He emphasized his statement by stabbing his sword into the wet ground next to him. The sword stood nearly as tall as he did.

"Han'Eiyuu," Gemini deduced. "I don't care about you. I want Shadowy Figure. If you'd rather be a villain, I don't care. But to go Rogue? To force your creator to change who you are? That is an abomination that I cannot allow."

Gemini reached behind him into the trusty C-space he had grown accustomed to using. He pulled out the same giant mallet he used to smash down the warehouse door in Supercity.

Han'Eiyuu laughed. "That is your weapon of choice? So be it!" The swordsman lifted his sword from the ground and struck a pose. The background behind Han'Eiyuu blurred into streaks of color, making him appear to be moving quickly even though he was standing still.

"That's neat," said Jimbob, "but what purpose does it serve?" He directed his question to Yuki.

"It's a speed pose," Yuki answered. "He's demonstrating how fast he can move."

"Why doesn't he just move fast to demonstrate how fast he can move?" Jimbob continued.

"Because," Han'Eiyuu growled, "this looks much cooler." He leapt into the air for an extended amount of time. Gemini looked up at him as the Rogue moved in slow motion, bringing his sword down with two hands in front of him.

Gemini watched him and took two steps to his left. Han'Eiyuu landed and missed with his maneuver. Gemini then swung his mallet sideways and knocked the swordsman over with a loud thunk.

Han'Eiyuu turned the fall into a roll and quickly popped back onto his feet. He tightened his grip on the sword and shouted, "SWORD AIR SLASH!" He cut his sword through the air, causing a powerful gust of wind that knocked Gemini to the ground.

Gemini struggled to his feet and picked up his fallen weapon. He responded with a shout of his own while leaping into the air, "MALLET GROUND SMASH!" He came down in front of Han'Eiyuu and pounded his mallet into the ground, causing a ripple wave of concrete, water, and other debris to strike the swordsman hard.

"This is getting exciting," said Jimbob the Talking Eggplant. He then pulled a lawn chair and a bag of popcorn from C-space and sat down. He offered some of the popcorn to Miss Fire and Yuki, both of whom declined.

"Why can't you accept what you are?" Gemini shouted at the Rogue. "Be the hero your creator designed you to be!"

Han'Eiyuu spat dirt from his mouth and wiped the back of his hand across his face, clearing off more dirt. "My creator filled my head with nothing but painful memories and anger. I already gained my revenge. My quest should be over, and I should be able to move on. Why am I forced to continue fighting as a hero, reliving my pain over and over again?"

A lightning bolt hit the stone steps of the temple, causing a huge spark and starting a fire at the base of the building around the fighters. Han'Eiyuu's dark eyes reflected the flames as he continued, "When the shadow man, Shadowy Figure, as you call him, gave me the key to changing my destiny, I decided I would inflict pain instead of live it. You're just one more victim!"

The swordsman charged Gemini with his long, thin sword held high. Gemini stood his ground as

Han'Eiyuu neared. The Rogue swung at Gemini, who timed a mallet strike to hit the sword instead of his opponent. The blade of the sword snapped in half, the pointed edge landing in the ground at Gemini's feet.

"My Masamune," the swordsman cried, staring at the broken blade in his hand.

"Well, Anchihiiroo," said the mallet-wielding champion. "You are defeated." Han'Eiyuu held his head down as he fell to his knees in the pooling water. "Tell me what you know about Shadowy Figure."

"Only that he plans to change Toonopolis forever and that we Rogues were just the first step." He lifted his eyes to Gemini. "Please end it. Finish me."

Gemini dropped his mallet to the ground. "No. You need to accept what you are, Anchihiiroo." He turned his back on his defeated opponent and walked away from the temple.

Jimbob jumped to his feet and applauded. "Now that's how you do it!" he shouted.

"Yuki, why did breaking his sword end the fight?" Miss Fire asked. "I've fought plenty of villains in Supercity, and destroying their weapons never led to surrender."

"We have different rules here, I guess," Yuki explained. "My brother's sword is more than just a weapon to him. It is his kindred spirit in battle."

Miss Fire nodded acceptingly. "So, it is his sidekick."

"But I bet it doesn't do laundry," Jimbob added with a smirk. The eggplant hopped quickly away from Miss Fire through the puddles of water to catch up with Gemini and avoid the superheroine's anger.

Miss Fire, Yuki, and Wan-Wan followed behind. When Jimbob caught up to his charge, Gemini stopped. "Where to next, boss?" asked the talking eggplant.

"To stop the last Rogue and try to figure out what Shadowy Figure could be trying to do that is even worse than what we've already seen. What could be worse than killing toons and creating Rogues?"

Jimbob shrugged. "I don't know, but hopefully we won't find out."

"So then, where are we headed next?" asked Miss Fire as she caught up to the two companions.

"Camenot," Jimbob answered. "There is one more known Rogue to deal with."

Yuki cleared his throat. "I want to help." Gemini looked sideways at the albino, who clearly was not a fighter. "Take Wan-Wan with you." The mechanical Akita barked in agreement. "He is more than just a pet. He can help you."

"Yeah, he can fetch us the newspaper and pee oil onto our enemies," Jimbob asserted.

Yuki smiled and whispered something into Wan-Wan's ear. A panel on the robot dog's side opened and a missile launcher appeared and pointed toward Jimbob.

"Ooh," Jimbob said, retreating backwards.

"Thank you," Gemini said, smiling as he reached down to pet Wan-Wan, who wagged his tail. The missile launcher retreated back inside the dog, and the panel closed. "What about you, Yuki? What will you do?"

The pale man raised his chin toward the temple they just left. "I am going to help my brother be who he was meant to be."

Gemini and his companions said their goodbyes. Gemini left Animetown with a new follower in tow and a stronger sense of purpose. The rain died down as they walked into a bamboo forest on the edge of the town, then made their way through the thick sprawling forest toward their next destination.

Chapter Nine

Camenot

Gemini and his crew emerged from a wooded
area into the rolling hills of a medieval
landscape. He looked back at the forest of thick
green trees and was amazed at how the bamboo
forest of Animetown seamlessly blended into the
pine forest of Camenot.

He turned back to look at the green hillsides.
On the highest hill stood a large castle with four
tall towers, one at each corner. The flags raised

and blowing in the country wind were black and bore a red sword.

Wan-Wan began his metallic barking at an approaching knight on horseback. The knight wore full black plate armor and carried a flag that was identical to the ones on the castle.

As the rider got close enough to hear the canindroid's threatening cries, he pulled back the reins on his ebony horse and he held up a hand in greeting. "I come bearing a message for the teenage champion they call Gemini," the knight said in a deep, booming voice.

"I am Gemini," the young man said, stepping forward to pat Wan-Wan, letting the mechanical Akita know to back down.

The knight dismounted, holding onto the reins to lead his horse toward the motley crew made up of a young man, a two-foot talking eggplant, a mechanical dog, and a woman dressed in fire-decorated clothing.

"Who are you and what message could you possibly have for me?" Gemini asked. "We've been in Camenot only a few seconds."

"Indeed, sir," the knight said politely. He removed his black helm and tucked it under his arm. His blond hair fell around his shoulders, contrasting vividly with his dark horse and armor. "Sir Goodypants has been told you were on your way. I am Hawk, leader of Sir Goodypants's royal knights."

Jimbob snickered. Miss Fire also seemed like she was trying to restrain herself from a giggle.

"May I ask what you find humorous?" asked Hawk to Jimbob.

"You serve a guy named Sir Goodypants?"

"Aye," said Hawk with no hesitation. "I serve a man who once was the most beloved paladin in Camenot. He asks that you seek audience with him at his castle to discuss your intentions in Camenot," he said to Gemini.

Gemini considered Hawk's words for a moment and rubbed his chin. "You said 'once was the most beloved.' He's not beloved anymore?"

Hawk cast his green eyes downward. "Not since he was bewitched by the shadow sorcerer."

Jimbob and Gemini exchanged wide-eyed glances. Jimbob's smirk immediately vanished from his face as he addressed Hawk seriously. "Shadowy Figure was here?"

"Is that your name for him?" Hawk scoffed. "Not was. He lives at Castle Camenot. Sir Goodypants met with him once and took him on, declaring he would no longer be Lawful Good. He declared his new alignment to be Chaotic Neutral."

"Of course," said Gemini. "Everyone wants to be Chaotic Neutral." He looked at Jimbob the Talking Eggplant and Miss Fire. "Looks like we found our Rogue."

Miss Fire scrunched her face and said, "I don't get it. What is this man talking about?"

Gemini explained. "Paladins are supposed to be unselfish saintly knights. They always follow the path of justice and righteousness. Lawful Good alignment means that they have to always do the honorable thing. This Sir Goodypants has changed to follow a selfish path that leads only to his own desires. Chaotic Neutral people are basically anarchists. They aren't really evil or good, they just do whatever they want to do."

Hawk nodded his head solemnly in agreement with Gemini's explanation. Jimbob reached behind his back and pulled out a handful of dice. He also put on a small T-shirt that read "I Roll 20s" on the front and "Dungeons and Dragons 4 Life" on the back. At a stern look from Gemini, he put the dice and shirt away as quickly as he had retrieved them.

Gemini addressed Hawk when he said, "And I suppose you and your compatriots are bound by your pledges of service to Sir Goodypants, even though he no longer follows the paladin's code?"

"You are exactly right, Sir Gemini," replied Hawk. "I am sorry, but we cannot break our vows, even if we now serve under a chaotic ruler." Hawk looked up at the sun in the sky. "Alas, we dawdle too long. We must hurry to the castle."

Gemini eyed the distance from their current position to the castle. "There's no way we can hurry there."

"Then ride with me. Your companions can catch up later. Sir Goodypants wishes to speak with you before the day is out."

Gemini was reluctant to leave behind his companions. Jimbob saw the dilemma and made a suggestion, "Just ride Wan-Wan there. Miss Fire and I will catch up."

Wan-Wan barked in response. Gemini eyed the robot Akita. "He's a big dog but not big enough for me to ride."

"Yeah, but he can transform!" Jimbob said.

Gemini scrunched his brow. "Yuki never said that."

"It says it right here in his manual," said Jimbob as he pulled from C-space a large tome labeled "Wan-Wan Instruction Manual." He held it upside-down and opened it to a random page. "He can turn into all sorts of stuff. His dog form is just his base. Lemme try."

Jimbob bounced over to Wan-Wan and lifted the panel on his side, revealing an array of buttons.

He pushed several of them with his conveniently appearing purple hand. Wan-Wan began to make whirring noises and quickly realigned his body into that of a large squirrel.

Miss Fire laughed at the sight. "So he's going to ride a squirrel instead?"

"Oops, wrong buttons." Jimbob looked over the manual, then flipped it so it was no longer upside-down. "Ah, that's better."

He pressed a new series of buttons on the squirrel's side-panel and Wan-Wan transformed into a majestic white metallic horse. Gemini's eyes widened as he looked at it, and Hawk's horse neighed in approval.

"Rainbow Bright, eat your heart out," said Jimbob.

"Yuki is amazing," Gemini said as he climbed up onto Wan-Wan the horse.

Hawk replaced his helmet and mounted his own ebony steed. He nodded at Jimbob and Miss Fire, turned his horse, and spurred it toward the castle. Gemini waved to his two companions and followed Hawk.

They rode swiftly through the countryside, barely giving Gemini any time to observe the surroundings. He hoped that Jimbob and Miss Fire would make it to the castle quickly since he had no idea what he would face there. The thought that

Shadowy Figure might be waiting for him was both exciting and terrifying.

At the castle, the drawbridge opened a path over the moat. They dismounted their horses at the stable. As a stable boy tried to take control of Wan-Wan, he transformed back into his dog form.

"Good boy, Wan-Wan," said Gemini as he patted the robot's head. "Stay here," he ordered. The dog sat down with a clank and accepted the order.

"Follow me, please," said Hawk. He led Gemini into a receiving room, where a tall man with white hair and piercing blue eyes sat at the head of a large rectangular table. He looked out over the table at an assembled group of men, all of who seemed reluctant to be there. They all wore medieval-style tunics matching the black and red flags of Sir Goodypants's castle.

"Ahh," cried the man at the site of Hawk and Gemini. "The child champion has arrived!" he announced in a jovial way, as far as Gemini could tell.

"Sir Goodypants, I presume," said Gemini, tightlipped.

"Indeed, Sir Gemini," he bellowed.

"And I am not a child."

Sir Goodypants laughed. "If you say so. I understand you have come to defeat me and restore Camenot back to its boring idealism."

"If that is what I must do to rid Toonopolis of Rogues, then yes."

Gemini balled his hands into fists and then reached behind his back slowly. Two of the men sitting at the table jumped up and grabbed Gemini's arms. Sir Goodypants laughed again.

"Let's not ruin the fun already, Sir Gemini. I don't think you appreciate how amazingly boring it is to be a paladin, never having any fun and always serving." For the first time since Gemini laid eyes on Sir Goodypants, the paladin's smile dropped. "I am not about to let you take that away from me just yet."

Unable to gain access to C-space, Gemini stopped struggling. He looked at Hawk, whose sad face Gemini read as regret. Gemini nodded at Hawk in affirmation that he understood.

"Well, Sir Goodypants," Gemini said as the two men released their grip on him, "what do you want then?"

"I want to propose a challenge," Goodypants said and returned the smile to his face.

"What is it?" Gemini asked through clenched teeth.

"There's been a new menace threatening my people and my castle, a wraith drake calling himself Phantasm. He has stolen some valuable possessions of mine, and I would like them back."

One of the men at the table leaned over to Sir Goodypants and whispered something to him. The paladin nodded and waved the man away.

"And apparently it's been eating villagers and stuff."

"And you want me to slay it?" asked Gemini.

Sir Goodypants nodded. "Oh, the noble young champion, so ready to thrust himself into danger for a just cause. You would have made a good paladin, Sir Gemini."

"That makes one of us," Gemini snapped back.

Sir Goodypants laughed. "Trying to appeal to my honor and pride, boy? No, that won't work. Before my new shadow sorcerer taught me how to change, I would have been bound to defeat the wraith drake myself. In fact, they would have written epics about me had I succeeded."

"And now?" asked Gemini.

"Now I am not so bound. I can send you to do it and take all the credit should you succeed. It makes a lot more sense, does it not?"

"For a coward it does."

"Now you're just being redundant," said Sir Goodypants. "I will, however, be noble enough to grant you a guide and one of my best warriors to assist in the task." He held pointed to Hawk, who had not moved since the conversation began.

"And what are the terms of your challenge?" Gemini questioned.

"Flee or fail, and I will have no choice but to take my army on an invasion spree to conquer other parts of Toonopolis." Sir Goodypants spoke with no humor in his voice and the men at the table seemed worried about this possibility.

"If I succeed?"

"I will tell you the next step of my shadow sorcerer's plan," he said, obviously not worried that he would lose the wager. "Do you accept my terms?"

Gemini walked toward Sir Goodypants. The men at the table moved to intercept him, but the paladin held up his hand to stay them.

"You must also agree to release your hold on your creator and return to your former self," Gemini demanded.

Sir Goodypants ran a hand pensively through his long white hair. He then smiled and offered his hand to Gemini. "You have a deal." Gemini and Sir Goodypants shook on the bargain.

Gemini turned away from the smiling Sir Goodypants and left the receiving room, Hawk following closely behind him. As they reached the open area of the castle, Jimbob and Miss Fire were entering through the lowered drawbridge. Wan-Wan barked and ran from the stables to greet them.

"Are we leaving already?" asked Jimbob.

Gemini nodded and explained the challenge set forth by Sir Goodypants regarding the slaying of the wraith drake. Hawk excused himself to prepare for battle while Gemini told the story.

"How do we know he will be true to his word?" asked Miss Fire.

"We don't," Gemini admitted. "But I find all of this very suspicious. I want to see what this wraith drake is all about. And if Sir Goodypants will not protect his people from this Phantasm, then I feel that I must."

"Why?" asked Jimbob.

"Because it's the right thing to do," Gemini answered succinctly.

Hawk returned from retrieving his battle gear. He was holding a black shield with a white hawk emblazoned across the front, a sword sheathed at his side. He had switched his showy plate armor for more breathable and flexible chainmail. His all-black armor still did not match well with his pure face and golden locks. He looked grim.

"Ooh, is the knight coming with us?" Jimbob gushed.

"Aye. Sir Goodypants has asked me to travel with you as a companion in the quest to slay Phantasm."

"Can I ride on the horsey?"

Hawk stared at Jimbob. Gemini laughed and Wan-Wan took the cue to transform back into his horse form.

"Hey, he responds to voice commands?" Jimbob asked rhetorically.

The stable boy brought Hawk's black horse to the knight and handed him the reins. Hawk mounted and trotted the horse toward Miss Fire. "Would the lady care for a ride?"

Miss Fire scoffed. "I'm no lady, knight. But yeah, I'll ride with you."

Jimbob frowned. "Guess I gotta ride on the metal horsey." Gemini mounted Wan-Wan, and Jimbob hopped up on the robotic horse as well.

Hawk rode slowly out of the castle. Wan-Wan followed with Gemini and Jimbob on his back. "The wraith drake's lair is not far from this castle," Hawk said as they crossed over the drawbridge. "We will be there shortly."

Jimbob turned to face Gemini. "You know this is a trap of some kind, don't you?"

"Of course it is. Haven't we already seen how predictable creations are? The Rogues follow a script, even if it is one they are writing themselves."

The rest of the ride toward Phantasm's lair was a quiet and morose one. Gemini agreed with Jimbob's feeling that it was definitely a trap of some sort. Still, he wanted to see it through to the end. He doubted that Sir Goodypants would keep his word even if he did succeed at the challenge. That would be an issue to tackle when the time came, however.

Hawk pulled up his horse outside of a cave, where tendrils of smoke from the mouth. It was clear that they had reached the resting place of the wraith drake, Phantasm. Hawk dismounted and helped Miss Fire down from the saddle.

Gemini jumped down from Wan-Wan's back as well, and Jimbob said, "Aren't you going to help me down like Hawk helped her?" He smiled wide.

"Nope," Gemini said.

"Some hero you are." Jimbob jumped down and landed on his face. Gemini helped the eggplant right himself. "Oh, now you help."

Gemini ignored his purple friend's complaints and approached Hawk. "What exactly is a wraith drake, anyway?"

"That might have been good to ask before accepting a quest to slay one," said Jimbob, brushing the dirt off his face.

"It is as its name implies. Not a mere dragon of flesh and scales, a wraith drake is an ethereal beast made of will-o'-the-wisps and smoke."

"Sounds lovely," Miss Fire said dryly. "How do we defeat it?"

Hawk's face stiffened. "No one has ever defeated one because this is the first one ever seen."

Jimbob hopped over to the group. "On that cheery note, I don't think we have time to figure it out." He pointed toward the entrance of the cave, where the smoke was thickening and getting darker.

Hawk adjusted his shield in front of him and drew his sword. Miss Fire ignited fireballs and held them in her hands. Gemini took out his trusty C-space mallet. Wan-Wan transformed from his horse form back into his dog form, with the added support of missile launchers popping out from his back.

In front of the prepared warriors, the wraith drake began to assemble. Amid the chaos of the smoke, a dragon-like shape began to appear. A pair of floating will-o'-the-wisps nestled in to become the eyes. As it settled into its final form, a rock flew over Gemini's head and sailed right through Phantasm.

Gemini turned around to look at Jimbob, who he assumed threw the rock. The eggplant shrugged and said, "Well, I'm out of ideas." He sat down on the ground.

The only effect that the rock-throwing incident had was to get the wraith drake to turn its attention on the assembled group and give vent a loud rasping roar. Wan-Wan fired a missile at its head, but once again, it went right through Phantasm and exploded against the side of the cave instead.

Phantasm roared again and belched a stream of black fire toward the adventurers. Hawk jumped in front of it and blocked the blast with his shield. As the fire subsided, Hawk tossed down the shield because it burned white hot from the flames.

"Let's see if we can fight fire with fire," the superheroine said and hurled balls of fire at the wraith drake. The fireballs landed several yards away from Phantasm.

"I guess Miss Fire's not a misnomer," said Jimbob. Miss Fire whirled on the eggplant with fire literally in her eyes. "Sorry, my mistake. I misspoke. I was misadvised by my brain."

"Are you quite finished?" shouted Gemini at his Toonopolis guide.

"Yes," Jimbob said sheepishly. "I'm sorry. I've been waiting since Supercity to say those things." He paused for a second. "I hope she doesn't mistrust me."

"That's it!" shouted Miss Fire. She turned to Jimbob, took two long steps, and kicked the vegetable like a football. He flew backwards about fifty feet away from the scene.

A throaty laugh came from within the wraith drake, forcing everyone's attention back onto it. Gemini shivered as he took some steps toward Phantasm, mallet raised.

"Nice to see how far you've come," the dragon said in a familiar raspy voice. Gemini's eyes widened in recognition. "Yes," said the dragon as it began to shrink. The smoke swirled around it until it resembled a more humanoid figure. His features were still obscured by the smoke and shadows, but he was undoubtedly the same person that Gemini first met in Adventure Realm.

"Shadowy Figure," Gemini said.

"The shadow sorcerer," gasped Hawk.

"Murderer!" cried Miss Fire.

"I did not realize how popular I was," Shadowy Figure said with a laugh.

"Hey!" Jimbob shouted. "It's Shadowy Figure." He trotted back to the rest of the group, flashing a cursory hurt glance at Miss Fire.

"I don't get it," Gemini said. "Why the ruse? What are you doing here pretending to be a dragon?"

"Just having a little fun, Gemini." Shadowy Figure continuously swirled and moved around, never taking a definitive shape other than his vaguely humanoid one. "I also needed to see how far you've come since our last little encounter."

"You're playing games with people's lives, Figure. You killed Plucky McGee's creator."

Shadowy Figure laughed. "I've only just begun!" He began to drift away.

"Where are you going? Stand and fight me!"

"I don't want to fight you yet, Gemini. I'm not quite recovered from our last little tryst, but I'll see you soon." Shadowy Figure quickly reformed into a smaller version of the wraith drake and took to flight.

"COWARD!" Gemini shouted after him.

"Come to Grayscale Village and see what type of power I can wield," Shadowy Figure called back over his shoulder as he flew away.

Gemini fell to his knees in frustration. "We were so close—"

"Gemini," Jimbob started, "we need to get to Grayscale Village. I don't like the sound of his threat."

Hawk, who had walked away to retrieve his shield, returned and joined the conversation. "Then we should begin our journey to this village," he said.

Miss Fire looked perplexed at the thought of Hawk joining them. She asked him, "Don't you have to serve Sir Goodypants?"

"Aye, m'lady. My lord commanded me to join you in your hunt for the wraith drake." He lifted his sword and pointed into the sky in the direction that Shadowy Figure flew. "I cannot return to him until that quest is complete."

"Hooray for loopholes!" cried Jimbob the Talking Eggplant.

The group—now five companions strong—gathered their various weapons and items. Hawk and Miss Fire mounted the black horse, while Wan-Wan reverted to horse form, and Gemini and Jimbob hopped onto his back. They rode away from the cave to follow Shadowy Figure's trail to Grayscale Village.

Agent Log: Project Gemini
Entry Number: 12
Date: July 1

In the last few weeks, only three more targets on the list given to our operative inside the Tooniverse were hit. Strangely enough, however, they were not stricken with Imagination Deficit Disorder like the previous targets. The three subjects in question were cursed with a much more normal version of insanity than the animalistic behavior brought on by the technique we trained our operative to use.

While I cannot express disappointment in the elimination of three more targets, it is concerning that the technique used by our operative to fulfill his mission has changed so drastically. It is unfortunate that I can only see the outward effects of his actions in the Tooniverse and not follow the events unfolding inside Toonopolis.

Also of note: one of the three aforementioned targets actually died from a brain embolism in conjunction with his insanity. I do not know if this was directly related to the actions taken by our man inside the cartoon universe or if was merely a happy coincidence. I look forward to debriefing Jacob Grenk once he returns to his full state of consciousness, but must complete his mission before I can do that. I have to admit that the suspense is growing in me.

Dr. James Grenk has fallen back in line with our plan after his previous detachment. Perhaps he remembered why he signed onto this project to begin with. More likely, though, it was my subtle reminder that even if he left the project, we still had control of his only child. I hate to be barbaric, but we have not usurped enough of his knowledge to continue Project Gemini without him.

I still feel like he is hiding something from us, but I can't quite put my finger on it. I have Dr. Kraft taking constant notes and attempting to delve into Grenk's computer files, but so far we have not turned up any sign of treachery. Call it my instincts but I feel we will eventually.

Special Agent Mimic
July 1

Chapter Ten

Grayscale Village

The group rested on one of the last hills of Camenot's territory. Sitting at the top of the hill, they had a great overhead view of Grayscale Village, a black-and-white little town that showed no signs of color. Clearly, the village was populated with classic animation-style cartoon creatures and buildings.

The four riders dismounted their steeds, Hawk and Miss Fire from the black horse, Jimbob and Gemini from Wan-Wan. Hawk whispered into the ear of the ebony stallion, and it trotted away from them, presumably back to Sir Goodypants's castle. Wan-Wan reverted back to his regular Akita form.

Unable to focus on the details of the village, Gemini frowned as he thought about how close he was to Shadowy Figure in Camenot. He didn't understand why the Figure would bait them simply to run away.

Jimbob the Talking Eggplant disrupted his thought process when he said, "I've been thinking."

Miss Fire and Gemini shared a groan at the notion of Jimbob thinking. They had both learned that it usually resulted in a bad pun or some other annoying routine.

"No, seriously," Jimbob protested. "About Shadowy Figure." He paused for validation.

"Just say it already," Gemini said.

"He has to be Jack Montana, don't you think?" Jimbob asked.

"It would make sense," Gemini agreed.

"Who is that?" asked Miss Fire and Hawk simultaneously.

Gemini and Jimbob shared their story of meeting the only other known Outsider in Toonopolis in the Warehouse Area of the city. They recounted his bizarre, paranoid behavior and the brief battle against some of his fighters from his cartoon battling company. Jack Montana obviously had a plan of some sort that involved the help of the Rogue named Angel, and he was extremely threatened by Gemini.

"The thing that I remember the most, though," said Jimbob, "is his claim that he was going to change Toonopolis forever. We heard the same thing from both Plucky McGee and that guy in Animetown."

"Anchihiiroo," Gemini supplied his name.

"Yeah, Anchovies," Jimbob sniffed. "I just don't imagine there's a ton of super-powerful beings running around Toonopolis trying to simultaneously change it forever."

Miss Fire nodded. "You know, Jimbob, for an idiot you can be pretty smart."

"Thanks!" Jimbob said, beaming.

"I agree," said Gemini, "but why the whole Shadowy Figure display? Why not just be himself? If he's that powerful of an Outsider, no one could stop him anyway."

"No one but you, m'lord," Hawk spoke up.

Wan-Wan barked in agreement.

Jimbob thought for a moment before responding. "Maybe he just likes putting on a show and making something of a game out of it?

We are talking about a guy who runs a cartoon fighting league."

A large crash that sounded like thunder interrupted their conversation. All of the members of the troupe turned their attention to the sky above Grayscale Village. They expected to see lightning, but the sky was darker than even the most ominous rain cloud.

As they watched, a black smoky whirlwind swept down from the darkness, turning into a tornado-like vortex. The dark wind swirled through portions of Grayscale Village, sending gray-toned pieces of the town all over the place.

Just as quickly as the tornado formed, it receded. The black cloud made only the sound of laughter as it floated away from Grayscale Village to an unknown destination. Gemini's group ran down the hill to assess the damage done by the short-lived black tornado.

Gemini stood on the edge of the town and could not quite figure out what he was looking at. In addition to the obvious oddity that all of the buildings, flowers, and trees looked like they were dancing, Gemini saw parts of the town that were purely black. Even in Grayscale Village, this didn't seem like it made sense. The black spots appeared to be black holes, as far as Gemini could tell. They bisected trees, houses, and other objects.

Grayscale Village

A gray-toned female squirrel in a sundress ran past the group, screaming. Gemini held up his hand to try to get the squirrel's attention, but she continued running, unaware of the visitors.

"What in Toonopolis?" Jimbob uttered as he surveyed the damage. The mysterious black spots were scattered throughout the village with seemingly no system or reason. Some of the buildings were only partially blacked out, but in some places, entire buildings had been replaced with the blackness.

Another gray-toned squirrel ran past them from the same direction. She looked identical to the first one. Gemini followed the squirrel as she ran past the dancing trees and noticed that the trees had smiling faces on them. He looked more closely at the greenery, or grayery, as it were, and the buildings. He noticed that nearly everything had smiley faces on it. They also still seemed to be dancing.

By the time the third squirrel ran past, it was clear to Gemini that she was actually the same squirrel just running in a circle while screaming.

"HEY!" Gemini shouted.

The squirrel finally stopped and looked at the full-color band of misfits from other parts of Toonopolis. Her eyes bugged, and she stared.

Jimbob walked over to the squirrel and waved a purple hand in front of her face, then looked back at his traveling companions and said, "Color shock?" He shrugged.

"Golly," said the squirrel.

"It speaks!" Jimbob cried.

"It speaks!" the squirrel replied. The squirrel looked at the two-foot talking eggplant as though she had never seen the color purple before. Gemini stepped up to speak to the squirrel, but she covered her eyes with a paw.

"What's wrong?" asked Gemini.

"The colors. Your clothes are so bright." The squirrel didn't remove the paw from her eyes.

Gemini looked down at his fuchsia pants and lime green shirt. Even in a colored world, they were bright and loud. He nodded his head, acknowledging the squirrel's assessment.

"Who are you guys?" asked the squirrel, peeking through her fingers. "Did you cause that tornado?"

"I am Gemini," he said. "I am an Outsider to the Tooniverse. We did not cause the tornado, but we are chasing the one who did." He turned toward the group. "These are my quest companions: Miss Fire from Supercity, Wan-Wan from Animetown, Hawk from Camenot, and

Jimbob the Talking Eggplant, my Toonopolis guide."

"I'm Macadamia," said the squirrel, finally able to take the paw from her face. Gemini felt her eyes must have been adjusting to the new colors, like when one wakes up to a bright light shining in one's face.

"Why are the trees looking at me?" asked Hawk, off-topic. "Are they possessed by spirits?"

"No, silly," said Macadamia. "All of the trees in Grayscale Village have faces."

"Why?" Hawk questioned.

Macadamia shrugged. "Beats me. And before you ask, I don't know why they dance either. They just do."

"So what was with the screaming?" Gemini queried to get back on topic.

Macadamia frowned and pointed to one of the larger spots of blackness. "My house." Her face drooped, and she began to cry.

"What did the tornado do?" asked Miss Fire.

"Painted everything black?" Jimbob answered with a question.

Macadamia shook her head. "That's what I thought too." She held up one of her paws that had previously been concealed. The tips of her fingers were pure black, contrasting with her gray-toned coloring. Wan-Wan sniffed at her fingers and growled.

"What magic is this?" asked Hawk.

"I tried to touch my house," she started, "or what was left in its place. I felt my fingers get absorbed into the blackness."

Gemini frowned and decided to get a closer look at the black space left in place of the squirrel's home. He and Jimbob walked toward the blackness, and the conversation continued behind him as the others followed.

"Did it hurt?" asked Miss Fire.

"It felt like nothing," Macadamia answered.

"So it didn't hurt?"

"No, but I don't know how to describe it," she said. "I felt my fingers there. Then I felt nothing, not even pain. Just . . . nothing."

Standing in front of the blackness, they tried to look around it from different angles, but they couldn't figure it out. It appeared to be a large black spheroid, as though the house and landscape were just shielded by a black circle.

"It's strange how there is still an outline to your fingers," observed Gemini.

The squirrel held her paw up in front of her. "I know. It's like they're there but at the same time they aren't. I can't move them. Golly, this is just bonkers."

"It sure is," agreed Jimbob as he gaped at the black spaces where Macadamia's fingers once were.

Gemini moved closer to the black sphere that stood where the squirrel's house once was and reached his hand out toward it.

"Stop!" Jimbob cried.

The boy paused with his hand slightly outstretched. "I need to figure out what this is."

"Well, do you want to end up like the fingerless squirrel?" Jimbob asked. He then looked at Macadamia. "Er, sorry. No offense."

"None taken," Macadamia responded.

"We don't know if it will affect me like it did her. If an Outsider like Shadowy Figure created this, maybe I can break through it. It might just be a barrier or something."

"Yeah, but," Jimbob struggled for an argument, "we don't even know for sure if Shadowy Figure is an Outsider. Maybe he's just a Rogue. We don't know."

"Weren't you the one who just argued that Jack Montana is probably Shadowy Figure?" asked Miss Fire.

Jimbob shot an angry glare at the superheroine. "Shut up, Misfit. Who asked you?"

"I did," Gemini said, defending her. "And I need to figure out what we're up against if we're going to try to defeat Shadowy Figure."

Jimbob drew a breath as though he would continue his argument but stopped short of talking. He sighed in resignation and waved his hand toward the black spheroid.

"It's your life, kid," he said.

"Right," Gemini agreed. "And you need to let me live it. You sound like my dad, Jeez."

Not waiting for Jimbob to respond, Gemini took another step toward the darkness. The gathered group of miscellaneous characters from different parts of Toonopolis held their breath collectively. Gemini reached out his hand and placed it against the black sphere.

"Aaaaaah!" screamed Gemini, pulling his hand back.

"What's wrong?" shouted Jimbob.

Hawk and Miss Fire ran toward Gemini and tackled him away from the darkness that had replaced the gray-toned squirrel's house. The three of them toppled to the gray earth. Underneath the pile, laughter could be heard.

"Is he laughing?" asked Macadamia.

Hawk and Miss Fire peeled themselves off Gemini, who was giggling loudly. "Just kidding," he said. "Nothing happened. It just felt like a solid wall to me."

"You're a jerk," said Miss Fire. "You've been hanging out with Jimbob too long."

Hawk said, "I agree with m'lady. 'Twas not a funny jest, sir."

Gemini stood up and brushed gray debris from his brightly colored clothing. "Okay, you're right. But everyone was getting so serious, I had to do something to lighten the mood." He walked back to the black circle and pressed both hands against it.

"How can you touch it but I couldn't?" asked Macadamia.

"Outsider," Jimbob, Hawk, and Miss Fire all said simultaneously.

"I can do a lot of things you creations can't do," Gemini added. "But it's more than just a barrier, I think. This whole sphere feels solid. I think the entire inside is filled with this same darkness."

He pressed his forehead against the darkness to try to look inside. The others all kept their distance from the circle, fearing a repeat of what had happened to Macadamia's fingers.

Jimbob ventured a little closer to address Gemini. "What do you think it is?"

"I don't know," he answered. "It's more solid than anything I've felt in the Tooniverse."

"It's nothing," called a voice from outside the gathered group.

"Well, that's helpful," retorted Jimbob. "Now that we know that, I guess we can go home."

Gemini's attention was drawn from the spheroid, and he looked past his companions at a creature that looked familiar. The gnome he'd met in the Field of Dreams was standing next to one of Grayscale Village's creepy face-bearing trees.

"Roy?" said Gemini.

The rest of the group followed Gemini's attention and stared at the little gnome who wore rainbow-colored clothes, complete with bow tie and pointy hat. He looked grimmer than Gemini remembered.

"Roy G. Biv, at your service," he said with a bow, smiling a clearly forced smile.

"What do you mean, 'nothing'?" Gemini asked.

"I mean the total opposite of everything, insofar as what is important to us here in the Tooniverse."

Miss Fire thrust a thumb at Roy G. Biv and said, "This guy makes less sense than Jimbob."

"I agree," said Jimbob. After a moment's pause, he added, "Heeey!"

Grayscale Village

"He makes perfect sense," argued Gemini. "What does everything in Toonopolis have in common?"

Gemini's companions looked puzzled, trying to figure out what the answer was, but no one had an immediate response. Jimbob started to say something twice but never finished a word.

"This isn't one of those 'why is a raven like a writing desk?' riddles, is it?" asked Jimbob finally.

"No. The answer is color," said the gnome who had been quiet since his last cryptic statement. "Everything in the Tooniverse has color. That . . ." he pointed to the black sphere, "does not."

Macadamia said, "Black is a color. Here in Grayscale Village, it's one of the only colors we have!"

Roy G. Biv shook his head, wiggling his rainbow hat in the process. "Not pureblack. Pureblack is the absence of all color. That's what you are seeing there. No color in the Tooniverse equals no existence." The comical-looking little gnome's somber face didn't remotely match his colorful attire.

Gemini walked to Roy G. Biv and kneeled in front of him. "So, Shadowy Figure is erasing toons? Is that how he has been killing them?"

Roy shook his head. "No," he mumbled. "Worse. An erased toon can be redrawn. He is absorbing them into himself. All of their color, everything that makes them who or what they are. In the process, he is also severing the connection between creator and creation. It can't be having a good effect on the creators."

"The fiend!" cried Hawk, raising his sword in the air.

"I think you might be even more upset when you see where he went after Grayscale Village." Roy sighed.

"Show us," Gemini requested. He turned to Macadamia and said, "I'm sorry for what happened here, Macadamia. I promise we'll try to set things straight."

The squirrel looked down at her blackened fingers. The rest of the group fell in behind Gemini.

"So, where did he go next?" asked Jimbob the Talking Eggplant.

"Stick Tent-City," said Roy G. Biv. "It isn't far from here. Follow me. It's the next section over from Grayscale Village."

Gemini and his companions followed the sad colorful gnome, leaving behind a sad monochromatic squirrel and the decimated Grayscale Village. The air around them was thick with fear at what they were about to see in Stick Tent-City.

Chapter Eleven

Stick Tent-City

As Gemini's crew approached Stick Tent-City, they could immediately see what Roy G. Biv was talking about when he said they would be more upset. The only thing that remaining was a gigantic black sphere like the one that covered the squirrel's house in Grayscale Village.

"Gasp," Jimbob the Talking Eggplant said out loud.

"I don't think you're actually supposed to say 'gasp'," suggested Gemini.

Jimbob audibly gasped in response. Miss Fire and Hawk stared at the large circle of pureblack that covered what they assumed used to be Stick Tent-City. Wan-Wan expressed all of their feelings when he whimpered and lay on the ground, covering his eyes with his large paws.

Roy G. Biv stepped in between the group and the remnants of the Tent-City, the pureblack behind him a stark contrast to the colorful clothing he wore. His face still bore a frown, also sharply contrasting with his happy-looking clothing.

"I came here as soon as I felt its destruction," said Roy.

"You felt it?" asked Gemini.

"You might say I have a special connection with Toonopolis," he answered. "I've been here since the beginning."

"Whoa," Jimbob started, "an Original?"

Roy G. Biv nodded.

"Wait, what?" said a confused Gemini. "Are you not a creation?"

"Yes and no. Am I the creation of a sentient being like the rest of the cartoons in Toonopolis? Yes." He paused. "Am I the creation of a human? No."

"Dolphin?" guessed Jimbob.

Roy snorted a brief laugh. "Closer, but not quite."

A coughing sound nearby derailed the conversation, shifting their attentions to a blanket on the ground that was moving in sync with the coughing. The blanket basically looked like a large piece of black paper. The upper portion of a circle-headed stick man appeared when the blanket shifted. The stick man blinked his small black-dot eyes. As he stood up, Gemini could see that the man was practically two-dimensional and paper thin like his blanket.

"What happened?" the figure asked groggily in a thick New York accent.

"Oh, nothing," said Jimbob. "Just that an entire section of Toonopolis has been absorbed and replaced with pureblack!"

The stick man turned his head toward what used to be Stick Tent-City. He shrugged his black-line shoulders. "I'd say it's an improvement, if ya ask me."

"Are you kidding me?" asked Gemini.

"Youse ever seen dis place before?" retorted the stick man.

"Well, no," Gemini said.

"Yeah, thought so. Fancy 3-D kid over here concerned about us little stick figures, huh?"

Hawk stepped toward the stick man and said, "I don't think I like your tone, sir."

The stick man spat on the ground next to him. "I don't t'ink I care what you t'ink." Hawk took a step closer to him. "Wanna fight about it?"

Gemini held up a hand to stay Hawk, who was conspicuously reaching for the hilt of his sword.

The stick man laughed, clearly not worried about getting assaulted by the large three-dimensional knight. "So what if Stick Tent-City is a big black hole now? No one cared about it before."

Gemini pondered the stick man's venomous thoughts. He looked out at the black sphere encompassing the former section of Toonopolis. He thought about all of the lives affected on Earth and elsewhere by the destruction of the creations inside the dark dome.

"Your creators care or you wouldn't exist," he said.

The stick man twirled a stick finger in the air nonchalantly. "Whoopdedoo!" he cried out. "Our creators couldn't even t'ink of us in three dimensions. How much do you t'ink dey really care?"

The stick man picked up his blanket, threw it over his shoulder, and walked away mumbling to himself and grumbling something about stupid creators and three-dimensional jerks. Gemini and his friends watched him disappear around the pureblack sphere.

"What a pleasant man," quipped Miss Fire.

"Can you blame him?" asked Jimbob the Talking Eggplant. "How would you feel if you were just a stick figure?"

Miss Fire looked pensive. "I'd feel however I was supposed to feel. That guy there is bordering on Rogue."

"I don't think so," said Gemini. "Seems to me his creator might just not like himself very much. I didn't get the Rogue vibe from him at all."

Gemini turned his attention back to Roy G. Biv, who was oddly silent during the encounter with the angry stick man. Roy had gotten closer to the pureblack orb but didn't touch it. His sad demeanor struck Gemini with a lament of his own.

"Why does this hurt you so much, Roy?" asked Gemini.

Roy took his attention away from the orb and looked up at Gemini. He said, "Lack of color hurts me. I live off color. In a way, I am color. It's hard to explain." He paused and took a breath. "What hurts most, though, is being powerless to fix it."

Jimbob hopped over to Roy. "I would think an Original would be pretty powerful, though. Maybe not as powerful as an Outsider like Gemini, but definitely stronger than a regular creation."

"And you'd think right, normally," said the brightly attired gnome. "Only the base of my power has been stolen by the Candemon."

"The what?" asked Miss Fire and Hawk simultaneously.

"The Candemon," Roy repeated. "He's taken over my homeland, Candy Island, and without my island, my powers are limited."

Jimbob said to Gemini, "Did he say Candemon? Seriously, that's one of the worst portmanteaus I've ever heard." He whispered for Gemini to hear, "I think your little gnome friend has lost it."

Gemini whispered back, "What in Toonopolis is a portmanteau?"

Jimbob continued to whisper, "You know, when you take two words and squish them together to make a new word, like brunch or spork."

Gemini shook his head at Jimbob then said to Roy, who clearly was still distraught, "Do you think Shadowy Figure had anything to do with the Candemon taking over your island?"

"I don't know," admitted Roy. "That creature has wanted my island for quite a long time, but never before has it actually attacked me. It was stronger than it should have been, even for an anomaly."

"Are you asking us to help you, Roy?" asked Gemini.

"I wouldn't have come to you if I thought you couldn't help me," he answered. "I've heard about your success with defeating Rogues. I know you seek Shadowy Figure and want to stop him from his evil ways. You're already becoming a hero in Toonopolis. Will you help me?"

"A hero?" Gemini mused.

"Aye, Sir Gemini, a hero you are," said Hawk.

"We wouldn't have followed you if you weren't, Gemini," Miss Fire added.

Wan-Wan barked and jumped onto Gemini happily, trying to lick him with his metal tongue. Gemini shooed him down. Jimbob smiled a very proud smile.

"I don't know that I'm a hero. I've just been doing what I felt was right," Gemini said. "Honestly, I never felt like I had a choice in my decisions."

Hawk, Miss Fire, and Roy G. Biv all smiled, and Wan-Wan even looked like he was smiling..

Jimbob bounced over and put one of his disappearing-reappearing hands onto Gemini's arm.

"I think that's the very definition of a hero," Jimbob declared.

Gemini frowned and pushed Jimbob's hand away. "I don't think you get what I'm saying. I don't mean that I did the right thing because it was the right thing to do. I feel no resistance to it."

"Like your mind is only giving you one option?" asked Jimbob.

"That's exactly what I mean. The little angel is on my shoulder but the little devil never shows up," Gemini said, trying to explain things in cartoon terms for the gathered group to understand. "That being said, I have no choice but to help you, Roy."

"Thank you, Gemini," the gnome said with a hopeful smile.

Jimbob raised his hand for his turn to speak. "What did you mean when you called the Candemon an anomaly?"

"I mean that he's a unique creature," answered the gnome. "You all know what a Rogue is, by now, considering your adventures up to this point."

They all nodded their heads to let Roy know that they knew very well what a Rogue was.

"Well, an Anomaly is kind of like that but much worse. You see, the Candemon's creator died years ago but still exists."

"How is that even possible without getting Terminally Moved?" asked Miss Fire.

Roy responded to Miss Fire's question with a question of his own. "Do you all know about the invisible thread that links a creation with its creator?" he asked.

Hawk and Miss Fire made faces that suggested they only somewhat understood. Gemini was likewise quiet. Only Jimbob gave any indication that he understood what Roy G. Biv was saying. He nodded an affirmative to the gnome's question.

"Well, it exists. And this creation managed to pull his creator's essence into the Tooniverse when she died, instead of letting it go. He keeps her essence alive inside of himself, refusing to release it and letting her die."

"He holds his creator hostage?" asked Hawk.

"Yes. That's what makes him an anomaly. Originals, Outsiders, Rogues—all of these are rare but not unheard of. The Candemon is truly one of a kind as far as I know."

"And the biggest perversion of the creator-creation relationships imaginable," added Jimbob in disgust.

"That is just sick," said Gemini. "Even if it were not a favor for you, it sounds like I'd still have to challenge this Candemon for the sake of its creator."

Gemini's companions all murmured agreement with Gemini's stance.

"Can I ask you another question?" Jimbob asked Roy seriously.

"You just did," Roy joked halfheartedly, "but you may ask me another if you want."

"Has there ever been the opposite of an anomaly? Has there ever been a creator who could follow the thread back to his creation?"

"Not that I know of," Roy answered. "For that to happen, the creator would have to know about the existence of the Tooniverse to begin with. I have only met one Outsider who returned to Earth with his mind intact. Most Outsiders either go crazy, die, or decide to stay here and live out their lives."

"Who did you meet?" Jimbob asked.

"Some special agent guy named Mimic, a very interesting person and quite a fast learner. He asked even more questions than you people," Roy said with a little grin.

"Okay, Gemini, are we ready to go to Candy Island?" Jimbob asked.

"I'm sorry, Roy, but no," Gemini said after a brief pause.

Roy frowned and asked, "Why not?"

"Before I can do that," Gemini began, "I think we need to visit Jack Montana in the Warehouse Area. If Jimbob is right and he really is Shadowy Figure, we need to put a stop to him before he can cause any more mass destruction like this."

He waved his arm at the pureblack sphere that had replaced Stick Tent-City. Roy G. Biv looked disappointed but resigned at the same time.

"I understand," said the colorful gnome. "When you are finished with what you must do in the Warehouse Area, meet me at the entrance to the Toonopolis Sewers. There is only one way we can get to Candy Island and it is through there."

"You won't come with us?" asked Gemini.

"I would be of no use to you without my powers," Roy said, shaking his head. "As it stands, I'm just a plain gnome in a silly outfit."

"You can say that again," joked Jimbob the Talking Eggplant with a smile.

"I'm just a plain gnome in a silly outfit."

"I didn't mean that literally," Jimbob said, his smile fading.

"Cartoons," mumbled Gemini, shaking his head as he walked away from the group.

The rest of Gemini's companions said their farewells to Roy G. Biv and followed their leader. They were all preparing for a showdown as they made their way back to the Warehouse Area to confront the Outsider that all evidence suggested was the deadly Shadowy Figure.

Chapter Twelve

Warehouse Area II

After a quick and uneventful journey through other sections of Toonopolis, Gemini once again found himself standing outside of a familiar building in Toonopolis's Warehouse Area. The gaudy Toonopolis Fighting World sign still lit up the otherwise abandoned-looking road. This time, however, Gemini was flanked by not only his Toonopolis guide, Jimbob the Talking Eggplant, but also his new friends Miss Fire, Hawk, and Wan-Wan.

The cartoon coterie looked up at the expansive warehouse in front of them, and Gemini braced himself for battle. If his last trip inside Jack Montana's warehouse was any indication, a fight was definitely impending. Gemini looked at his assembled companions and smiled, feeling that he was much more prepared to confront Jack Montana than he was the last time he was here.

"Thank you guys for coming," said Gemini to his friends.

"To the ends of Toonopolis, Sir Gemini," responded Hawk.

Wan-Wan barked and wagged his tail with its mechanical whirring sound.

Miss Fire put her hand on Gemini's shoulder and said, "You have been there for us, kid. Now it's time for us to be there for you."

"Insert additional sappy sentiment here," said Jimbob the Talking Eggplant. All eyes swept onto the two-foot eggplant, who put on a goofy grin. "Just trying to lighten the mood," he mumbled under his breath.

Gemini laughed. "I never know whether to hug you or punch you in the face," he admitted to his guide.

"I can accept that," Jimbob said with a shrug.

"Well," started Gemini, "last time we were here we tried a surprise approach to Jack Montana and it led us nowhere."

"That may be because his surprise approach consisted of us wearing mustaches and pretending to be delivery people," pointed out Jimbob.

"Well, if Superman can become Clark Kent with a pair of glasses," said Miss Fire.

"That's what I said!" Gemini yelled.

"Who is Superman?" asked a confused Hawk.

"Never mind," said Jimbob. "What's the plan this time?"

Gemini paused and thought for a moment. He assessed his team and peered back at the warehouse that may have contained the powerful Shadowy Figure, who had caused so much turmoil in Toonopolis since his arrival.

"I say we just bust in, defeat whatever is in our way, confront Jack Montana, and wring the truth out of him," he said finally.

"Sounds a little complicated," joked Miss Fire. "I'm not sure Jimbob can handle that plan."

"Blah blah blah blah blah," responded Jimbob. "I'm sorry, Miss Fire, did you say something?"

"Very mature, Jimbob," said Gemini. He looked around at each of his companions and nodded. "Everyone ready?" he asked.

The warriors all prepared themselves in their own ways. Wan-Wan opened up his side panels to prepare his missiles, Hawk readied his shield and sword, Gemini took out his giant mallet from C-space, and Miss Fire lit up her hands with flames.

Gemini glared at Jimbob. "Ready to fight?"

"Erm," Jimbob said. "I'm more of a thinker than a fighter."

Gemini simply blinked at Jimbob.

"Moral support character?" Jimbob ventured. "Plucky sidekick?"

Miss Fire shot him an evil glance, seemingly remembering her fallen comrade, the sidekick named Plucky McGee.

"Sorry," said Jimbob sincerely. "Bad choice of words." Jimbob reached into C-space and brought out a book labeled *Fighting For Dummies*. The group collectively groaned and gave up on expecting any physical support from Jimbob.

"Let's do this," Gemini urged his cohorts.

He nodded to Miss Fire, who cast a large fireball at the door to the Toonopolis Fighting World warehouse. The whole team sprinted toward the building. As the entranceway to the warehouse quickly went up in flames, a large figure loomed behind the fire. They froze as the shape quickly morphed into the cyclops that Jimbob and Gemini

faced the last time they tried to meet with Jack
Montana.

The cyclops stepped through the flames and
roared at the intruders that had torched his
employer's door. The four fighting members of
the group were preparing for an altercation when
they heard a whooshing sound over their heads.
Gemini looked up and saw a book flying through
the air. It connected directly with the cyclops's
eye, driving him to his knees in pain.

Gemini turned around to look at Jimbob the
Talking Eggplant, who no longer was holding his
Fighting For Dummies book.

Jimbob smiled and said, "Chapter Two: if you
can't fight, throw things at your enemy and hope
for the best!"

"I'm afraid to ask what Chapter One said."

"When in doubt, kick your opponent in the
groin and run," Jimbob supplied. "I skipped that
chapter." He looked down at his rounded bottom.
"No feet."

"Makes sense," Gemini conceded. "But we're
just beginning," he said, turning his attention back
to the cyclops.

The cyclops was recovering from his book-to-
the-eye injury and getting to his feet. He retrieved
his large club and dipped it into the flames behind
him, leaving him wielding a flaming club.

"Beware the flaming club o' doom," said the cyclops in a thick Irish accent. He sported a grin that revealed only a few teeth.

"Beware the sword of justice," cried Hawk as he charged at the cyclops. The one-eyed giant swung the flaming club at the righteous paladin, who deftly deflected the blow with his shield, ducked a return swing, and drove his sword into the cyclops's foot, pinning him in place.

Gemini saw the opportunity created by Hawk's assault and ran into the fray with his mallet held high. The distracted monster was focused on trying to free his foot when Gemini's mallet smashed him in the chest, sending him rolling into the fire at his back.

The warriors and Jimbob seized the opportunity to leap through the flames and into the warehouse, leaving the cyclops behind them roaring in pain as it attempted to flee the fire. Along the way, Hawk retrieved his sword from the giant's foot.

As they entered the warehouse, Wan-Wan turned and fired a missile at the doorway, causing an explosion that filled the entranceway with rubble. Gemini gave him a nodding approval for blocking the possible return of the cyclops. They continued down the hallway that Gemini and Jimbob were led through during their last visit.

As they rounded a corner, they came face to face with a snarling Venus flytrap. Gemini felt that this would not have been alarming if it were not for the fact that the flytrap had a face, arms, and legs. It was also over six feet tall. That it was, in fact, snarling also posed a concern to Gemini. He didn't recall any stories of snarling carnivorous plants in his high school biology class.

"You will never get to my master," the flytrap said in a woman's voice. "Venus has never been defeated."

"Oh?" said Gemini. "Well, how about a little fire, scarecrow!" He ducked as Miss Fire hurled two flaming bursts toward the plant creature.

Venus screamed as the flames lapped at her body. Then she began laughing. "Don't you know that living plants don't catch fire very easily?" she mocked. She then spat a gob of sticky green mucous at the heroes. Hawk attempted to block it with his shield, but the mucous merely dispersed and stuck to them all.

"Which one of you tasty morsels should I sample first?" she asked seductively. Her eyes fell on Gemini, and she walked slowly toward the would-be hero, who struggled to free himself from the sticky substance that had them all trapped.

As she bent over to place her huge mouth around Gemini, the sound of a dog barking broke the dead air. Wan-Wan had used his mechanical devices to free himself and was leaping to block Venus's attack on Gemini. Not realizing the robot dog was freed, Venus snapped at Gemini and swallowed Wan-Wan instead.

The remaining members of Gemini's crew stared in shock as Venus took a step back and swallowed their robotic friend. She smiled and said, "A little too much iron for my taste but delicious nonetheless."

"You demon!" cried Hawk. "Release Wan-Wan!"

"Oh, I don't think that will happen," she cooed at him. "It's been so long since I've had a proper meal. I am only allowed to incapacitate toons in this league, but never digest." She frowned. "But enemies of Mr. Montana? Fair meal."

She began to laugh when Gemini heard a faint mechanical sound from within the giant flytrap. Gemini smiled and raised a hand to wave at Venus.

"Why are you waving?" she demanded.

"Just saying goodbye," Gemini said through his grin.

An explosion replaced the Venus flytrap, causing a green splatter to burst in three hundred sixty degrees from where she once stood. Wan-Wan was left standing in the wake of her destruction, the remnants of a large bomb the only evidence of Wan-Wan's plan.

"Good boy!" Gemini shouted to the canindroid.

Wan-Wan traveled in turn to each of the companions and worked on freeing them from Venus's sticky trap. He seemed very excited at all of the positive feedback he was receiving.

"I love that dog," said Jimbob the Talking Eggplant as he was freed. He bounced toward a nearby door. "This is the door that led us to the pit where we fought last time we were here."

"Let's hope Jack Montana is waiting for us again." Gemini walked through the doorway.

This time, the fighting pit was already lit up and there were no surprises waiting for them. Instead, Jack Montana was sitting on the bleachers at the edge of the fighting pit looking at them as soon as they walked in. The Rogue known as Angel sat in a chair next to him. The pale lanky man stood and applauded.

"Boy you are persistent, Gemini," he said. "You really should join me, you know. We could rule Toonopolis together."

"I want nothing to do with you, Shadowy Figure," Gemini spat out accusingly. "Or with the way you want to change Toonopolis forever."

For the first time in the two meetings Gemini had with him, Jack Montana's eyes widened in surprise. He began laughing maniacally and clapped his hands together. "Oh, that is so wonderful!" he said through his crazy laughter.

"What's wonderful?" asked Gemini, both confusion and wariness in his voice.

"You've been coming after me because you think I'm Shadowy Figure?" He laughed again and ran his hand through his thinning hair.

Angel laughed as well and spoke for the first time. Her voice was deep and sultry, like a soul singer's. "You think Jack has that kind of power? Ha!" she said. "You must be crazier than he is."

"Yeah!" agreed Jack Montana. "Hey, wait a minute."

"Don't play dumb with us, Montana," said Jimbob. "Only an Outsider would have the power to do what Shadowy Figure has been doing to Toonopolis. You and Gemini are the only two Outsiders here."

"Correction!" Jack said with a squeal. "We are the only two *known* Outsiders. Besides, I have no interest in destroying Toonopolis. I love it here. In fact, I hate that guy. He's a jerk."

"What?" asked Gemini.

Angel stood up, her wings and other parts bouncing up and down in the process. "Let me explain it to you, kid." She waved her arm at Jack Montana like a game-show valet. "Look at him. A pale, balding, thirty-something loser on Earth can actually be something here."

Jack Montana shook his head in agreement.

Angel continued, "Why would he want to destroy a place that offers him his only chance at greatness? Here he can be anything."

"I understand that all too well," said Gemini. "But what is all this talk about 'changing Toonopolis forever' and why does he keep sending toons to attack us?"

Angel shrugged. "In case you haven't noticed," she said, "Jack's a little nuts."

"I object to that statement!" Jack Montana shouted. Angel rolled her eyes at him. "I am more than a little nuts!" he finished with a laugh.

"You want to know what we're changing and why I teamed up with Jack?" Angel asked.

Gemini nodded, still baffled by the sudden turn of events unfolding before him. Angel reached behind her and tossed something down at Gemini. He caught a cold pint container of ice cream and looked at the label. He looked up at Angel, who nodded.

"'Uncle Jack's Frozen Yogurt'?" he read from the carton. "Frozen yogurt? That's his big plan?"

"Yes," Jack Montana said. "And I would have gotten away with it too if it weren't for you meddling kids and that dog!"

Wan-Wan turned his head to the side with a confused whine. Miss Fire patted him on the head to comfort the mechanical dog's confusion.

"Got away with what?" asked Jimbob. "We don't care if you're starting a brand of frozen yogurt."

"So, you aren't here on a mission of industrial espionage to steal my secret recipe?" asked Jack with a frown. He actually seemed like he was disappointed about it.

"Why in Toonopolis would we want to do that?" asked Gemini.

"Because it's tasty!" replied Jack Montana.

Gemini sat down on the ground, kicking up a cloud of dust from the fighting pit floor. His shoulders slumped and his face was distraught. "I thought for sure . . ." he mumbled.

"What's his problem?" asked Angel in an uncaring tone.

"We seek to destroy the shadow sorcerer, but we have no more leads, m'lady," said Hawk.

"Ooh, m'lady? A gentleman, eh? Whatcha doing later, Sir Knight?" Angel asked with a wink.

"Serving my lord, Sir Goodypants, and assisting Sir Gemini in his quest to defeat the shadowy menace," Hawk answered.

Angel looked disappointed. "A paladin, huh? No use barking up that tree."

"Maybe we should give up," Gemini said dejectedly. "We don't know anything else about Shadowy Figure. If Jack is not who we were looking for, what do we do now?"

"If I may, m'lord," Hawk offered. "We have pledged our support to Sir Roy in his quest to retake his Candy Island. He awaits us at the Toonopolis sewers as we speak."

Gemini stood up and brushed the dirt off his fuchsia pants. He straightened his face. "You're right, Hawk. Thank you for reminding me. We still don't know about this Candemon and why he suddenly became powerful enough to oust an Original from his home."

Jack waved at Gemini. "Bye kids! Have fun storming the castle."

Gemini gave one last look at Jack Montana and Angel and shook his head in amazement. He had felt for sure that Jack held the answer to his Shadowy Figure dilemma.

Toonopolis: Gemini

Gemini gathered his troops to exit the Warehouse Area and meet with Roy G. Biv at the Toonopolis Sewers. He had thought that his mission was nearly over and was suddenly faced with the reality that it might still be near the beginning.

He decided not to be daunted by the reality of his situation and to press forward with the same level of excitement he had possessed this far into his journey. Even though he was dejected to discover that Jack Montana was not Shadowy Figure, Gemini moved onto the next leg of his adventure with the hope that he and his companions could still be successful in stopping Shadowy Figure's destruction of Toonopolis.

Agent Log: Project Gemini
Entry Number: 16
Date: July 29

I am bothered to report that there seems to have been a large snag in our plans under Project Gemini. While the cases of Imagination Deficit Disorder were originally rare and targeted, the last month or so has revealed a widespread epidemic that has caught the attention of the mainstream media.

Where once only neuroscientists studied the few cases of IDD that existed, the general public is now aware of it. I've even heard that they have their own awareness ribbon-puce, I think.

This can only mean one of two things, and both of them are not good for my project's success. The first possibility is that my agent inside Toonopolis has gone rogue and has started attacking individuals not on the target list. This is the best-case scenario.

The worst-case scenario is that I have competition inside the Tooniverse, and someone else has discovered our method and is applying it more haphazardly than the Agency. If this continues for much longer, I may have to recall our agent and debrief him on the happenings in Toonopolis.

I mentioned this possibility to Dr. Grenk, and to my surprise, he actually suggested that we continue the project and leave his son in the Tooniverse for a while longer. I found this very strange, considering he had been petitioning to retrieve his son's essence for several months now.

When I questioned his change of heart, he only said that he had a feeling that extracting his son from the Tooniverse at this time might prove more dangerous than leaving him inside. He was unable to provide any sufficient data to back up this feeling and stated that it was just an instinct.

Against my own instincts, I have decided to allow our operative more time inside Toonopolis, at much professional risk to myself. Dr. Grenk better hope that his instincts are more right than my own in this situation, or the ramifications will be great.

Special Agent Mimic
July 29

Chapter Thirteen

Toonopolis Sewers

Just as he had promised, Roy G. Biv was waiting at the entrance to the Toonopolis Sewers for Gemini and his troupe. Roy was sitting patiently on top of a manhole cover that, conveniently, was on a street not too far from the Warehouse Area. When Roy saw Gemini and the rest of the group, the gnome smiled widely, stood up, and straightened his oversized rainbow-colored bow tie.

"Welcome, friends!" he cried. "How did your trip go? Did you find Shadowy Figure?"

"No," said a dejected Gemini, his shoulders slumped low. "Jack Montana was just a whack-job trying to start a frozen yogurt brand using Angel to advertise it."

Jimbob the Talking Eggplant held up a carton of Uncle Jack's Frozen Yogurt. "It's sinfully delicious!" he shouted.

"Are you serious?" asked Miss Fire, rolling her eyes.

Jimbob feigned being hurt. "You have to admit, that's a clever tagline for the yogurt, considering who Montana is using as the spokesperson."

"I hate you sometimes," she responded.

"It hurts my feelings when you're mean to me like that," said Jimbob with a sniffle.

"It hurts my head when you talk half of the time. Why does it seem like you have two different brains in that purple head of yours?" Miss Fire asked.

"Maybe because there is!" he shouted and laughed maniacally. "Seriously, though, I know something you don't hate," Jimbob added after abruptly stopping his laughter. He held up the carton and continued, "Frozen yogurt. No one hates frozen yogurt."

Gemini groaned and turned his attention from Jimbob to the gnome standing on top of the sewer entrance. "So, we are here to fulfill our promise to you. Shall we?"

Wan-Wan approached the manhole and sniffed at it. He let out a yelp and covered his nose with one of his paws. Roy nodded his head knowingly.

"It isn't the most pleasant of entranceways, I'll admit. Fortunately, I've never had to use it before today," said Roy G. Biv.

"Wait," Miss Fire said, sounding concerned. "You've never gone this way before? How do you know where to go?"

"Well, as I understand it, all drains lead to the ocean. My island is in the ocean. It's pretty much a connect-the-dots scenario from there," said Roy with a tentative smile.

"Makes sense to me," said Jimbob, his mouth full of frozen yogurt.

"Sir Roy, how did you used to get to your island?" asked Hawk.

"I just used my magic to teleport there," Roy answered. His smile downgraded from tentative to nonexistent. "But now—"

"We know," interrupted Gemini. "You have no powers. That's why we're going to get them back. Wan-Wan, if you could please?" he asked, pointing to the sewer.

Wan-Wan whined but still used his tail to lift the manhole cover out of the way. A green tendril of gas escaped from within the entranceway to the tunnel. Jimbob peered over the edge of the hole and nearly vomited.

"Ladies first?" he ventured, turning his head to Miss Fire.

"I don't think so, veggie-boy," she responded. With a swift motion, she pushed Jimbob into the hole with her foot.

"AAIIEEE!" shouted Jimbob as he fell. Miss Fire turned her ear to the hole and counted silently until she heard a splash at the bottom.

"It's not that far down," she stated.

"There's also a ladder," Roy said, pointing to the side of the open tunnel.

Miss Fire shrugged with a smile. The group climbed down the ladder into the sewer below. As they assembled at the bottom, a sopping wet Jimbob the Talking Eggplant was bouncing angrily out of a river of foul-smelling sewer water, his cheeks a shade of reddish-purple.

"Look," said Miss Fire, "he's hopping mad!"

"Oh, look who has to say her own bad puns without her sidekick around," Jimbob snarled.

Hawk and Gemini tried to control their laughter. Roy G. Biv didn't even try. The colorful gnome fell to the ground laughing while Jimbob stared at them all, then he laughed too.

"Okay," he admitted, "that was pretty funny." He narrowed his eyes at Miss Fire and made an I'm-watching-you motion with his fingers. "But you are a very mean super-lady. And I will not be sharing my yogurt with you."

"I'm heartbroken," Miss Fire said through her laughter.

Gemini took a look around the sewer and noticed two different tunnels. Water flowed equally through them both, so it was not simple for him to decide which way they should go.

"I think we should split up," Gemini suggested.

"Are you sure that is wise, Sir Gemini?" asked Hawk. "We have come this far with a combined effort."

"Well," Gemini said, "if all drains lead to the ocean, both of these tunnels will lead us to our destination. We just don't know which one is faster. Whichever group gets to the island first gets first shot at the Candemon."

"Ah-ha," said Hawk with a glint in his eye. "A challenge it is, then!"

"Sure," said Gemini, smiling at Hawk's enthusiasm. "Why don't you take Wan-Wan and Miss Fire down the left tunnel. I will take Jimbob and Roy down the right."

The two groups assembled at the entranceway to their respective tunnels. The superheroine, the knight, and the mechanical dog stood at the left. The Outsider, the guide, and the powerless Original stood at the right.

"Don't you think these teams are a little unfair, kid?" asked Miss Fire. "We have three fighters. You have yourself, an eggplant, and a gnome. This isn't a gardening competition."

Gemini simply pointed a thumb to himself and smiled. "Outsider," he said. "It's more than fair."

Hawk bowed to Gemini and grinned. "We shall see you on the other side, m'lord."

The two teams waved to each other and set off into their respective tunnels. Gemini led the way down the right with Jimbob the Talking Eggplant and Roy G. Biv close behind. They traveled next to a green-tinged waterway, following the flow of the liquid.

"Ooh, look," said Jimbob, pointing to a faint green glow in the distance. He bounced ahead of Gemini, forcing the Outsider to follow quickly behind. Roy G. Biv struggled on his tiny legs to keep up.

"It's a turtle," Gemini said as they arrived at the green glow. "And it seems to be walking around in radioactive waste. That doesn't seem very safe." Gemini attempted to divert the three of them away from the scene.

"Wait," called Roy G. Biv. "Something is growing on it!"

"It's probably a tumor," responded Gemini. He turned back to the turtle just in time to witness a second head pop out from the shell next to the original head. "Yeah, we should go," he said.

"I have to try something, first," Jimbob said with a grin. He bounced over to the turtle and said, "Mr. Turtle, how many licks does it take to get to the Tootsie Roll center of a Tootsie Pop?"

Jimbob laughed at his joke until the head on the left replied, "I never made it without biting."

"However," said the head on the right, "don't go ask the owl. He's a candy thief."

"Ooh-kay," said Jimbob as he slowly backed away from the mutated turtle. He turned to Gemini. "Yeah, let's get out of here."

Gemini and his two companions walked away from the mutant turtle, continuing to follow the trail of the sewer river. They soon reached a part where the water changed color from its green-tinted hue to a grayish tone.

"We must be under Grayscale Village," Roy G. Biv observed. "Isn't it neat how the waste even matches?"

"Yes," agreed Jimbob. "Grayscale poop is so much less disgusting than regular poop."

"Poot," a voice said that didn't belong to Gemini, Jimbob, or Roy.

Gemini looked across the monochromatic river and saw a gray cloud staring back across at him. The cloud had two wide eyes but no other obvious facial features. It blinked at them.

"Aww, look how cute!" Jimbob called out. "What did that girl in Animetown say? Kaway?"

"It's kawaii, Jimbob," corrected Gemini. "And no, it isn't cute. It's a gray fart cloud."

"Poot-poot-pfft!" said the cloud as it floated toward them.

Gemini and Roy backed away as the cloud approached. Jimbob stayed and smiled at the cloud as it flew closer. "What's your name?" Jimbob asked the cloud.

"Poot!" the cloud responded.

"Poot, eh? What a great name."

"Jimbob, I'm not sure its name is Poot. I just think that's all it can say," Roy G. Biv suggested.

Jimbob dismissively waved off Roy's suggestion and said, "I'm going to call you Poot."

"PFFT!" said Poot, who appeared happy at the attention.

"Do you know the way to the ocean through the sewers, little guy?" asked Jimbob sweetly.

"Poot-poot-poot!" said the gray cloud excitedly, widening its eyes in agreement.

"Can you lead us there?"

"POOT!" said Poot. The cloud began floating above the gray-toned river, leading the adventurers farther down the tunnel.

Gemini stared at Jimbob the Talking Eggplant in amazement. "You are a genius," he said.

"Half the time," agreed Jimbob with a grin.

"Well," said Gemini, "follow that Poot!"

They followed Poot along the river until the gray coloring of the water slowly gave way to a green-tinted hue again. The silent lapping of the sewer water against the pathway was also slowly replaced by a louder sound of rushing water. After a few more moments, the rushing gave way to a crashing as the group stood on the edge of the tunnel, staring down at a huge drop-off.

"It's a sewerfall," observed Jimbob.

Poot continued to float through the air and ended up on the other side of the precipice before turning around to see that the others were not following him. "Poot-poot-poot!" it cried out excitedly.

"I think it's saying that the exit is right over there," deduced Roy G. Biv.

"Poot!" Poot said in agreement.

Gemini peered down over the edge of the sewerfall. "I don't see any way down here. I also don't see any way back up the other side."

"Hey, Rainbow-boy, can't you make us a rainbow to cross or something?" asked Jimbob.

"If I had my powers, yes," Roy said. "But in case you forgot, our goal is to go get them."

"It'd be a lot easier to get your powers back if we already had your powers," grumbled Jimbob.

"Yes?" responded Roy, a befuddled look on his face.

"I think I know how to get across," said Gemini suddenly. "Gravity Effectiveness Displacement."

Jimbob looked confused.

Roy's eyes widened and he smiled. "That's perfect," he said. "But can you do it?"

"What is 'it'?" asked Jimbob.

"In cartoons," Gemini began, "have you ever noticed how the toons don't fall off a cliff until they realize they are no longer standing on it?"

"So you want to run off the cliff and hope you don't fall?" asked Jimbob. Gemini nodded. "And you guys think I'm the stupid one," he murmured.

"Actually," Roy said, "it can work. The trick is to just not know when the ground ends and you can run right across. It's quite the paradox."

Jimbob nodded knowingly. "I agree. A pair of ducks would be very helpful. We could just fly on their backs to the other side."

Roy G. Biv and Gemini simultaneously smacked themselves in the face with their own hands. Ignoring Jimbob's statement, Gemini began to size up the chasm between the tunnel they were in and the exit marked by Poot. He nodded his head and took several steps back from the edge of the tunnel.

"Here goes nothing," Gemini said.

He closed his eyes and ran full-speed toward the edge of the tunnel, trying to clear his mind and think about anything other than the fact that he was running off the edge of a cliff. He focused on Shadowy Figure and how strongly he desired to defeat him. He thought about the destruction he saw in Grayscale Village and Stick Tent-City.

"Poot!" Gemini heard cheerfully next to his ear. He opened his eyes and realized that he had traversed the divide and was standing right next to the wide-eyed, gray cloud. He turned around and waved to Jimbob and Roy.

"You did it!" cried the colorful gnome. "My turn," he added gleefully. He mirrored Gemini's actions and ran, eyes closed, across the divide.

Gemini watched the gnome cross the space between the two sewer drop-offs, amazed that he had just done the same thing himself. Roy soon and stood next to Gemini and Poot.

"Your turn, Jimbob," said Gemini.

"I don't like this idea. Can't you guys just come back for me later?" Jimbob peeked over the edge of the sewerfall.

"I can't go ahead without my guide," Gemini pleaded. "You can do it, Jimbob."

"I guess," said the eggplant, unconvinced.

He followed the same steps that Gemini and Roy G. Biv had taken, backing up and running toward the sewerfall with his eyes closed.

Gemini watched as Jimbob made it halfway across the divide before he opened his eyes and looked down.

"No!" cried Gemini.

Jimbob immediately fell toward the bottom of the chasm. "It wasn't me; it was the one-armed man!" Jimbob screamed as he fell.

"Poot!" shouted the gray cloud and dove off the edge of the tunnel toward Jimbob. It became a streak of gray with the speed it traveled as it caught up to the falling purple eggplant. Poot dove beneath Jimbob just before he hit the ground, and the talking eggplant landed on the cloud with a soft thud. Poot flew back up to Gemini and Roy G. Biv with Jimbob riding on top of it.

"Thank you, Poot," said Jimbob as he jumped onto the ground next to Gemini. "You saved my skin, little buddy."

"Poot-pfft-poot," said Poot, who nuzzled next to Jimbob.

"But please stop touching me," Jimbob continued disgustedly. "You smell like poo." Poot's eyes drooped. "But you're still my buddy! Just a buddy from a distance."

Poot seemed to accept this. It then motioned for them to turn around. Gemini turned and saw daylight. The tunnel in which they were standing poured out directly into the large blue ocean. Gemini smiled and Roy appeared hopeful.

"We made it to the ocean, Roy," said Gemini. "Where to next?"

"Underwater City is not too far from the shore. I'm sure someone there will be able to help us get to my island," replied the gnome.

"We have to go underwater?" complained Jimbob.

"Yes," said Roy. "Is that a problem?"

"I've heard that soaking an eggplant in salt water removes the bitterness," Jimbob said with a worried look on his face.

"Oh?" replied Gemini with a grin. "In that case . . ." He picked up Jimbob and hurled him into the ocean. Gemini turned to look at Poot, whose eyes widened with surprise. "He'll be okay, Poot. Thank you for your help."

"Pfft-poot!" replied Poot.

Gemini looked back to the ocean and dove off the edge of the tunnel into the salty water. Roy G. Biv followed close behind.

After they had drifted to the bottom of the ocean, they saw Jimbob the Talking Eggplant staring angrily at them. Roy G. Biv pointed over Jimbob's shoulder to a glimmering light in the distance under the water. Gemini knew he was directing them toward the underwater city ahead and began trudging through the silt at the ocean bottom toward the city's lights, expecting his angry guide to follow.

Chapter Fourteen

Underwater City

As Gemini, Jimbob, and Roy G. Biv approached the lights of Underwater City, Gemini realized that he did not need to hold his breath under the water. He glanced at Jimbob and Roy, who also appeared to be breathing normally, albeit with small bubbles occasionally rising to the surface from their mouths.

"How are we breathing?" asked Gemini. Roy and Jimbob turned to look at him. "And how do you guys hear me underwater?"

"The magic of cartoons," said Roy. "Much like the Gravity Effectiveness Displacement trick, you will only drown in water if you think you will."

"Or if it's funny for you to drown," added Jimbob.

"Exactly," the gnome agreed.

Gemini shook his head and continued walking toward Underwater City. After a few more steps, he tripped over something and tumbled to the bottom. A cloud of silt rose over him as he struggled to get to his feet. He tugged at his foot and found it stuck inside a pineapple.

"Why would there be a pineapple under the sea?" asked Gemini.

"Why, indeed?" echoed Jimbob the Talking Eggplant.

Gemini kicked off the offending pineapple and stood up. The group resumed to its trek toward the city. As they approached the outskirts, Gemini realized that something was wrong.

"Oh no," cried Roy G. Biv. "I thought we left this destruction at Stick Tent-City."

Gemini saw that the pureblack spheres that plagued Grayscale Village and Stick Tent-City encompassed portions of Underwater City. The sections of the city that were not damaged by the spheres were physically destroyed, leaving piles of coral rubble strewn about the ocean floor.

"Psst," whispered a female voice from behind a large rock.

Gemini saw a young pink-haired girl peering from behind the rock. When he walked over to her, she ducked from view.

"What happened here?" he asked the girl.

He rounded the rock and noticed that she was not an ordinary girl. Her human upper half wore only a coconut-shell bikini, and her lower half was a sleek pinkish color that ended in eight tentacles instead of feet.

"Holy Toonopolis!" cried Jimbob the Talking Eggplant and fell over at the sight of the octopus-girl.

"Oh come on now," sighed the girl. "You've never seen an octonoid before?"

"Not one that wasn't deep-fried," admitted Jimbob. Roy G. Biv came from behind Jimbob and smacked the eggplant in the back.

"Ignore Jimbob, Princess Polipo," the rainbow-clad gnome said.

"Roy!" she cried. She swam quickly toward the gnome and tackled him into the ocean bottom, causing a cloud of debris to float up around them.

Underwater City

As the dust settled, Princess Polipo was streaming tears and hugging Roy G. Biv.

"What happened, Polipo?" he asked. "Where is your father?"

"The Candemon sent swarms of its minions down at us. He also had some mysterious shadowy guy with him. Father tried to defend Underwater City, but there were too many of them. He was taken by the Candemon's gummy sea creatures back to Candy Island."

"What about Shadowy Figure?" asked Gemini.

"He was horrible. He attacked random parts of our city with those black orbs. Every time Father and our guards would make progress against the gummy creatures, the shadowy man would take out an entire section of our defenses. His laugh was horrible, like it was just a game to him."

"There, there, Princess," Roy said, trying to soothe the octonoid. "We're here to help." He tried to smile for her but was obviously distraught.

"We saw lights when we were approaching Underwater City," Gemini said. "If the city is destroyed, where were the lights coming from?"

"I think them," Jimbob said, pointing to the middle of the city. Gemini looked where Jimbob was pointing and saw a large group of gummy worms, occasionally sparking as though they were electrical.

"Are those . . ." Gemini began, ducking back behind the rock. The rest of the group followed him.

"Gummy eels," Princess Polipo answered. "They've been left to search the city for anyone who still survives. Everyone else who wasn't eaten by the black orbs was taken to Candy Island."

"I wonder what the Candemon wants," Roy said.

"I know what it wants," Polipo admitted.

Gemini looked at Polipo's sad eyes. "Well?" he asked, trying not to sound too insensitive.

"He sent a message before the attack," she said. "He said that since he was now King of Candy Island, he needed a queen. My people were trying to protect me."

The octonoid princess started crying again. Roy G. Biv hugged her and patted her on the shoulder. "Now, Princess, don't cry too loudly or they will have failed. So far, they've been able to keep you safe."

"At what cost?" she shouted in a whisper. "I would have rather sacrificed myself than my entire city, including my father."

"Well," said Roy, "knowing King Ochopatas, he would strongly disagree with that." He smiled. "But don't worry, Polipo, for I have brought with me a great hero who has already agreed to combat the Candemon on my behalf."

Roy G. Biv waved his arms toward Gemini, who smiled meekly at Princess Polipo and waved.

"He's a great hero?" asked Polipo.

"He sure is," said Jimbob defiantly. "He's already kind of defeated three rogues and an Outsider, as well as survived two encounters with Shadowy Figure."

Polipo hid her mouth with her hand and whispered to Roy G. Biv, "Gee, the criteria for hero-status seem to be dropping, eh?"

"Princess, Gemini is an Outsider and a very powerful one, at that. Don't let his looks deceive you or his eggplant friend's stupidity concern you."

"Yeah," said Jimbob in agreement. Gemini assumed he only heard the first part of Roy's last statement.

"So how do you 'kind of' defeat people?" asked the Princess.

Gemini started to speak but was interrupted by Jimbob who said, "One Rogue was dying when we got there. One Rogue he just had to break his sword to defeat. The last Rogue we never actually fought nor did anything about. We didn't fight the Outsider either, just his creation employees. And

Shadowy Figure ran away from us twice, only the first time it was after he made Gemini pass out."

Jimbob took a deep breath after spitting Gemini's adventure out in rapid succession. Gemini stared at Jimbob and blinked.

"Wow," he said, "you make it all sound so heroic. Look, Princess, I never called myself a hero and I don't plan on starting now. All I really want to do is find Shadowy Figure and try to get the rest of my memories back."

Princess Polipo nodded her understanding.

Gemini continued, "Along the way, I seem to have made some people think I'm something more than I am for whatever reason. I haven't been able to resist helping people who ask me for help and that is why I'm here now."

Roy G. Biv smiled and pointed a thumb at himself, acknowledging that he was the one who had asked for help.

"But truthfully," Gemini added, "now that I know for sure that the Candemon and Shadowy Figure are connected, I am even more looking forward to defeating the Candemon to get to Shadowy Figure. I won't lie and claim I am a hero, but I do have power and I fully intend to destroy the Candemon and to set its creator free."

"I like your honesty," said Polipo as Gemini finished his speech.

"I like your coconuts," said Jimbob to Polipo. The octonoid smacked Jimbob with all eight of her tentacles and both of her hands in rapid succession. "What'd I say?" he cried out after the assault.

"Will you lead us to Candy Island?" Gemini asked, ignoring Jimbob as he had become accustomed to doing.

"Doesn't Roy know the way?" asked Polipo.

"Sadly, Princess, I don't," Roy admitted with a frown. "I always just used my magic to teleport places, including here. I don't know my way anywhere, it seems. We came here to see if someone could help us."

"I can lead you there," Polipo said, "but it won't be easy. The Candemon has his gummy creatures all over the place. Can you swim?"

Gemini and Roy G. Biv affirmed that they could swim, while Jimbob the Talking Eggplant looked down at his legless bottom and frowned.

"I don't think eggplants were made for swimming," he said.

"Just climb on my back," Gemini said. "You weigh practically nothing."

Jimbob climbed onto Gemini with a grin on his face. "I haven't had a piggyback ride in a long time. Giddy-up, horsey!"

"I might change my mind and feed you to the gummy eels," an annoyed Gemini said, shaking the eggplant off his back.

Jimbob frowned as he climbed back onto Gemini. The teenager gave Polipo a thumbs-up, and the octonoid princess swam upwards. Gemini and Roy G. Biv followed. Princess Polipo led them closer to the city, trying to keep them obscured from the sparking eyes of the gummy eels.

"They can't see very well in the dark," Polipo whispered. "That's why they keep having to light up."

The group swam as quickly and silently as they could around the outside of the city, using the debris of the fallen buildings and the pureblack spheres to prevent themselves from being seen. They soon found themselves on the opposite end of Underwater City, where Gemini noticed a strong current of water in front of him.

Princess Polipo nodded toward the current. "We just need to ride this. It will take us right to the beaches of Candy Island."

Gemini followed the octonoid into the strong stream of water, and he felt a sharp pull on his body as the tide swept him away from the devastated Underwater City. Jimbob released his hold on Gemini's neck and was pulled along as well. Roy G. Biv quietly tailed the group.

After what felt like a short ride, the current shot the group out and back into calmer waters. Gemini looked back and was surprised to see that the city was no longer in view. "How far did we travel?" he asked Polipo.

"About three leagues."

"Oh, well, that helps," said Jimbob sarcastically.

"It's about nine miles," Roy added.

Gemini opened his mouth in shock. "We were only in the current for a few seconds. How did we go so far?"

Polipo shrugged her shoulders and said, "It's a strong current."

Gemini turned away from the current and looked ahead. He could see the bottom of the ocean begin to slope upward, suggesting that it was turning into a beach not too far away. He smiled and began to swim toward the shore.

"Watch out!" cried Roy G. Biv, grabbing Gemini's hand and yanking him backwards. He pointed to a school of red fish swimming nearby.

"What? It's just a few fish," Gemini said.

"Those are no ordinary fish," Princess Polipo pointed out. "Those are Swedish piranhas. And they're swarming the coastline."

"Can we fight them?" asked Gemini.

Polipo shook her head. "There are far too many of them. Even if you are as strong as Roy says, you're in their element and outnumbered. You'll have to sneak through the Cave of Despair."

Jimbob's eyes went wide with fear. "Oh," he said, "sounds lovely. Sign me up."

"It's either that or try to get through the Swedish piranhas," Polipo said.

Gemini and Jimbob looked at each other and then back at the red fish. As they weighed their options, one of the fish bumped into two others. The two fish that were struck bared their sharp teeth and tore the other fish into pieces within seconds. The rest of the fish continued on course as though nothing had happened.

"Cave of Despair it is!" cried Jimbob.

Roy nodded grimly and motioned for them to follow him. They swam toward the surface and then away from the shoreline to a side of the island that was flanked by a sheer wall. Gemini knew immediately that they couldn't climb the wall.

"Where is the cave?" he asked Roy.

"It's underwater. It leads into the center of the island and comes out at Licorice Lagoon."

"I know I'm going to regret asking this, but why is it called the Cave of Despair?" Gemini asked the gnome.

"An ancient evil called Gumthulu sleeps in the cave. It feeds on fear and suffering and has slept there since as far back as I can remember."

Roy motioned for them to head back under the water. The rocky cliff continued straight down to the sandy ocean floor, a small dark opening at the base where the two met.

"Why would such an evil creature live under your Candy Island filled with rainbows and lollipops?" Jimbob asked seriously.

"Two sides to the same coin," Roy G. Biv answered cryptically.

"Like a chocolate candy coin?" Jimbob asked.

"No," Roy answered. "We are opposites, Gumthulu and I."

Gemini nodded solemnly. "I get it," he said with a grim smile. "You can't have hope without despair. Is Gumthulu an Original like you, Roy?"

"Yup," said the gnome. "I just hope he's still sleeping. With all of the fear and despair generated by Shadowy Figure and Candemon, he might be growing stronger and less dormant."

"On that note," said Princess Polipo, "I wish you guys good luck."

"You aren't coming with us?" Gemini asked the octonoid princess.

"I have to try to find survivors in Underwater City. Also, I won't be much help to you once you get to the lagoon," she added, shaking her tentacles at him. "Not much for going on land, you see."

Gemini understood and wished her farewell. Jimbob and Roy G. Biv also said their goodbyes. Princess Polipo swam back to the other side of the island, and the three remaining placed their eyes on the entrance to the Cave of Despair.

"It's very important that we maintain hope as we go through this cave," said Roy. "If Gumthulu senses fear, he might awaken."

"Then maybe you should have called it the Cave of Happy Fluffy Bunnies and told us there was ice cream and milkshakes waiting on the other side," said Jimbob the Talking Eggplant.

Gemini thought for a moment about Jimbob's suggestion and then responded, "But wouldn't the bunnies drown underwater?"

Roy agreed, "Yeah. That wouldn't make for very happy bunnies."

"I hate you people," Jimbob grumbled. He waved a purple hand toward the Cave of Despair. "Shall we, then?"

The trio crept toward the opening in the underwater rock face, taking them one step closer to the Candemon and, Gemini hoped, Shadowy Figure. He was nervous about traveling through the Cave of Despair but tried to follow Roy's advice to stay hopeful. He found this hard to do while he was entering the lair of an ancient evil creature. As he stepped into the mouth of the cave, he was unfortunately only able to picture drowned bunnies. He was not sure that this boded well for their trip through Gumthulu's domain.

Chapter Fifteen

Candy Island

The three companions walked as silently as they could through the dark cavern that led to Licorice Lagoon on Candy Island. Gemini feared that they would awaken the evil Original, Gumthulu, and he tried to calm his fears, remembering that fear itself could wake the beast.

"How far do we need to go?" Gemini asked Roy G. Biv.

"I don't think it's that far. Licorice Lagoon is in the very center of the island."

They continued forward, groping along the walls. Darkness crept in around them the farther they went into the Cave of Despair. After a short time, Gemini was no longer able to see in front of him at all. He stopped, and Jimbob the Talking Eggplant and Roy G. Biv bumped into his back. They all fell to the ground in a succession of thuds.

"I think I bent my stem," cried Jimbob.

Gemini untangled himself from his two small friends and stood. "We are going to need some light. How are we supposed to sneak past this thing if we can't see? We might just walk right into it."

"Is this where we fire up a torch underwater somehow?" asked Jimbob the Talking Eggplant. "And after we do that, we realize that we're standing right next to Gumthulu and wake him up?"

"Light won't wake him up," Roy said.

"And why not?" asked the eggplant.

"Gumthulu has been living in the dark for so long that he is blind. He can't see anyway."

Gemini smiled for the first time since entering the Cave of Despair. He reached behind his back and pulled out an old-fashioned torch, fully lit despite being underwater.

Jimbob scoffed at Gemini and mumbled, "Showoff."

"You gave me the idea," Gemini said through his smile. "But now that I know we don't have to worry about light waking him up, we just need to be quiet."

Gemini motioned for Roy and Jimbob to follow him as he continued through the cave. He was glad that he was now able to see where he was going, and it made it much easier for his spirits to remain high. After walking along the lone corridor a while, they reached a four-way intersection. Gemini awaited direction from the gnome.

Roy walked to the center of the intersection and stuck his nose in the air. He sniffed at each of the paths and paused to think.

"I know it's not this way," he said, pointing to the path on their left. "That way smells like peppermint, not licorice. But the other two both smell like licorice."

"Maybe they both lead to Licorice Lagoon," Gemini offered.

"It could be," Roy said.

"Then let's go right," Gemini decided. He turned down the path to their right, urging Roy and Jimbob to follow.

"So," Jimbob began, "do we actually have a plan for when we reach the Candemon?"

"Sure do," Gemini answered.

After another moment of silent walking, Jimbob sighed and said, "Well?"

"Kill the Candemon. Free its creator. Find out where Shadowy Figure is hiding." Jimbob stared at him. "What?" Gemini asked. "That plan worked in the Warehouse Area against Jack Montana's fighting toons."

Jimbob began to object to the vagueness of Gemini's plan, but Roy motioned for him to put his hand down. Jimbob silently objected to Roy's suppression by way of sticking out a purple tongue at the gnome.

The group fell into silence again with the only sounds being the occasional air bubbles escaping from their mouths and noses. Gemini followed the underwater cave's path. He suddenly stopped and took a step backwards, knocking over Jimbob, who was still glaring at Roy.

"What the hey!" Jimbob cried as he fell over.

"Shh!" Gemini spat out. "Look," he whispered.

In front of them was a large face that looked like the head of a giant squid. Its eyes were closed, and it breathed lightly as though it were asleep. The pink-skinned creature blocked the entire pathway, and Gemini could smell a strong waft of licorice coming from it.

Gemini's eyes widened. He turned to Roy and asked quietly, "Gumthulu?"

Roy nodded silently.

Gemini turned his back to the sleeping giant and began to slowly tiptoe toward the intersection. Roy followed him just as quietly. Jimbob did not turn. He, instead, kept his eyes fixed on the enormous creature in front of him.

"Jimbob," Gemini whispered, "come on. We need to get out of here."

Jimbob did not respond. Gemini walked back to his eggplant friend and reached out to grab him. Upon doing so, one of Gumthulu's pink eyelids suddenly popped open. The eye that was revealed looked like a large red gumball with a small black iris in the middle.

"Uh oh," said Roy from behind Gemini.

"Jimbob! Snap out of it!" Gemini said. He slapped the talking eggplant in the face, which seemed to do the trick. Jimbob became suddenly alert. "We have to get out of here, like now!"

Candy Island

Jimbob looked at Gemini and then back at the creature that was stirring. The eggplant seemed to finally realize what was happening and began hopping away. After a few feet, he stopped.

"Come on, Jimbob," called Gemini.

"I have an idea!" he said and turned back toward Gumthulu.

Gemini watched in horror as Jimbob crept up to the squid's face and reached out his two purple hands toward the giant Original. With a move swifter than Gemini had ever seen his purple friend use, Jimbob leapt toward Gumthulu and snatched his eye from the socket.

"Yoink!" cried Jimbob, hefting the eye that was as large as himself over his head. He hopped quickly past Gemini with a devilish grin on his face.

Gemini shook off his disbelief and ran to catch up with the bouncing eggplant. Roy followed along as quickly as he could. The trio reached the four-way intersection again and quickly turned to the right. They bolted down the pathway, expecting Gumthulu to come charging from behind at any moment.

"What were you thinking?" cried Gemini between gasps.

"I wasn't!" Jimbob said, laughing. "I just figured it would be fun."

"Fun to anger a sleeping evil?" asked Roy from a few feet behind them.

"Fun to grab a big gumball out of a giant squid's eye socket," Jimbob corrected. "And yell 'yoink.'"

"You said you had an idea," said Gemini.

"I did!"

Jimbob hopped faster than he ever had before. Gemini raced after him, partly to get away from Gumthulu and partly to try to catch the little eggplant to strangle him. He was so focused on running that he didn't see what was ahead of him until he was standing in the center of a ring of light streaming from above.

"Licorice Lagoon!" cried out Roy G. Biv.

The three of them quickly swam to the surface and pulled themselves onto the black grass next to the water, the air redolent with the strong smell of licorice. Gemini panted as he stretched out on his back and turned his head toward Jimbob, who was leaning over the giant red gumball-eye of Gumthulu.

"That was very uncharacteristic of you," Gemini pointed out.

"Maybe I'm more complicated than you thought," Jimbob said with a knowing smile. "Maybe you aren't the only hero around here."

"Or maybe," Roy added as he got to his feet. "Maybe you were just so overtaken with fear that you lost your mind."

"You can't lose something you don't have," Gemini joked.

Jimbob laughed and hoisted his trophy above his head. Gemini looked at the eyeball and shuddered. He patted Roy on the shoulder and smiled at him.

"How can you guys just laugh at this?" Roy asked.

"If you can't laugh, you might as well be dead," said Jimbob. Gemini looked sharply at Jimbob and his grin faded. "What?" asked the eggplant.

"My mother used to say that all the time."

"Then she was a wise woman!" Jimbob decreed. "Now may I suggest we get far away from here in case that thing wants its eye back?"

"Yeah, good call," Gemini agreed. "Where to, Roy?"

Roy shook off his concern about his two friends' nonchalance and looked around. He pointed toward a group of trees that had many different colored bean-shaped objects hanging from them.

"If we cut through Jellybean Jungle, we can get to the path that leads to Taffy Towers, my home."

"Then let's be on our way," Gemini said.

Jimbob hefted up the eye of Gumthulu and began hopping toward the jungle. Gemini sighed.

"What?" asked Jimbob.

"Would you throw that thing back into the lagoon? You aren't seriously planning on carrying it for the rest of our journey, are you?"

The sad look on Jimbob's face told Gemini that he was, in fact, planning on carrying the eye for the rest of their journey. He pouted at Gemini like a kid who was about to lose a toy.

"Oh, fine," Gemini said. He walked over to Jimbob and took the eye from him, then he reached behind his back and placed the eye into C-space. "You can have it back when our adventure is over."

Jimbob lowered his eyes. "Yes, sir."

"Good boy," Gemini jested. "Now let's go slay us a Candemon," he said as they entered the Jellybean Jungle.

Gemini looked up and was amazed at all of the different colored jellybeans that were growing on the trees. He plucked a red one from a low-hanging branch, popped it into his mouth, and quickly spat it out.

"Ugh. I hate getting cinnamon when I'm expecting cherry."

Candy Island

Roy laughed and jumped to grab a red jellybean of his own. He handed it to Gemini. "You have to be able to tell the difference between the shades of red."

Gemini ate the cherry jellybean happily. "Roy, will Gumthulu follow us?" asked Gemini seriously.

"If he hasn't already, he probably fell back asleep."

"Even after Captain Genius plucked out his eye?"

Roy nodded. "Only fear will waken the beast. He doesn't feel pain. He started to wake up because of Jimbob's fear. When he overcame the fear and took the eye, Gumthulu probably just fell back asleep."

"Good thing I went past scared and into crazy," Jimbob said with a smile.

"Good thing, indeed," Gemini agreed.

They made it through the jungle faster than Gemini expected. Either the release of the fear of Gumthulu quickened their steps or the jungle simply wasn't that large. Gemini emerged from the jellybean trees and felt a familiar crunch under his feet. He smiled as he looked down at the Rainbow-PEZ Road and recalled when he first met Roy G. Biv.

"It seems so long ago that I first stepped onto this road," Gemini said. "I don't think I ever thanked you for leading me into Toonopolis, Roy."

"No thanks needed, Gemini. I often help lead confused toons into the city. It can be crazy if they don't get sorted properly."

"Holy giant towers of taffy," blurted Jimbob the Talking Eggplant.

Gemini followed the eggplant's gaze and saw Taffy Towers, an enormous rainbow-colored castle at the end of the Rainbow-PEZ Road. There were seven giant towers positioned like a seven-pointed star. Each tower was painted one of the seven colors of the rainbow. Countless tube-like walkways connected the towers above a rainbow-colored field of grass. From what Gemini could see, the Rainbow-PEZ Road led right to the center of the colorful spectacle.

"Wow," was all Gemini could say at the sight.

Roy G. Biv sighed as he gazed upon his home.

"Are you okay, Roy?" Gemini asked.

"I am. I just miss it. So many beautiful colors. So much joy. It's so hard for me, being sad since the Candemon took my home. It's against my very nature to be sad."

"It's against my nature to be brave, but I did it back there anyway!" decreed Jimbob proudly.

Gemini scoffed at him. "I think the coward-to-hero change is a little less noble than the happy-to-sad change, don't you?"

"That's besides the point," Jimbob whined.

"Anyway," started Gemini with a smile, "there's no reason to be sad anymore, Roy. Let's go get your home back!"

Roy beamed at Gemini. When Gemini saw Roy's smile grow wider, he felt a surge of confidence. He nodded to his two diminutive companions and began marching toward Taffy Towers. Gemini felt an air of purpose as they neared Roy G. Biv's home.

They followed the Rainbow-PEZ Road as it ran between the yellow and green peaks of Taffy Towers, and Gemini's muscles began to tense for a confrontation. He noticed a throne at the end of the road that was plastered with all of the colors of the rainbow. Next to the throne sat a very large water tank.

"I don't think I like this place," said Jimbob. "It looks like Mother Nature ate a bag of Skittles and then threw up."

Gemini ignored Jimbob's comments and addressed Roy G. Biv. "Where do you think we'll find the Candemon?"

"I thought he'd be on the throne," Roy replied.

"What's with the water tank?" asked Jimbob as they neared the throne.

"It is for my future wife," said a hollow-sounding voice from behind them. They all turned toward the voice at once.

Gemini saw the Candemon for the first time. He wasn't sure what he expected the Candemon to look like, but it certainly wasn't what he saw before him. It was a hodgepodge of pieces of candy thrown together.

Its arms were candy canes, its torso a giant, upside-down gummy bear. It had chocolate bars for legs and a candy apple for a head. There were inconsistently placed hard candies of varying colors for its eyes, nose, and mouth. Gemini wasn't sure how it walked, let alone spoke. He also noticed an out-of-place-looking necklace made of different-shaped crystal prisms draped around the stick-neck of the Candemon.

"Okay," said Jimbob, "I think I'm gonna be sick looking at this thing."

"Now, that hurts my feelings," said the Candemon.

"Furthermore," Jimbob continued, "I would have to say that Candystein or Frankencandy would have been a much better name for it."

"I'm right here, you know."

"Hmm, maybe Piecemeal or Haphazard."

"That's it!" roared the Candemon. It opened its mouth and spat out a wad of melted marshmallow onto Jimbob the Talking Eggplant. The marshmallow engulfed the eggplant immediately. Gemini ran to his guide's side and reached out to try to remove the marshmallow but found that it had instantly hardened around Jimbob.

"Nice trick," said Gemini coolly. "You actually got Jimbob to shut up."

The Candemon laughed. Even its laugh sounded hollow to Gemini. "Welcome home, Roy," the creature said mockingly. "Is this your champion?" He pointed one of his candy-cane arms at the boy in fuchsia and lime.

"I can speak for myself, Candemon," Gemini said, stepping between the creature and the gnome. "I'm here to set your creator free and kill you once and for all."

"Is that so?" A golden glowing orb sparked inside the gummy-bear stomach of the Candemon, and Gemini heard a twinkling noise from within the bear. "Shut up, you," the Candemon spoke to its stomach.

"But first you are going to tell me where I can find Shadowy Figure."

"I think not."

The Candemon spat out another wad of marshmallow, and Gemini dove to his right to avoid the molten sugar. He tried to rise and realized that the marshmallow had hit his left foot, pinning him to the ground. The Frankenstein-esque candy monster, its hard-candy mouth in a twisted grin, walked awkwardly toward the prone Gemini.

"How pathetic," it said. "You traveled all this way only to get defeated so easily? I'm actually a little disappointed."

The anomaly placed one of its candy-cane arms into its mouth and giggled. When it removed the arm, it was filed to a sharp point. The Candemon stood above Gemini and prepared to strike when it lost its balance and toppled over Gemini's body. Gemini smiled as he saw Roy G. Biv clutched to the back of the Candemon's head, scraping at the crystal necklace it wore.

"The necklace!" cried out Roy G. Biv. "It's the source of my powers."

The Candemon reached behind with its unsharpened arm and snatched the rainbow-clad gnome from his perch, threw Roy to the ground, and turned back toward Gemini, who was frantically trying to escape from his marshmallow trap. Roy lay on the ground motionless.

Candy Island

"And what a pretty necklace it is," the hollow voice of the Candemon mocked. The creature raised its pointy arm to stab at Gemini, who winced and prepared for the blow.

THUD! THUD!

Gemini opened his eyes and saw two arrows sticking out of the gummy bear torso of the Candemon, who was stunned. Gemini turned his head and saw something in the air that made him smile.

"Hawk! Wan-Wan! Miss Fire!" he shouted. His traveling companions had finally made it to Candy Island. The paladin Hawk and the superheroine Miss Fire were riding on the back of a flying Wan-Wan, whose four robot-dog legs had jet bursts streaming from them.

Wan-Wan hovered to the ground and landed with a thump. Hawk and Miss Fire quickly leapt off his back and ran to Gemini. The Candemon roared and ripped off the shafts of the arrows, leaving the tips embedded in its gelatinous chest.

"You didn't think we'd miss out on this fight, did you, kid?" said a smiling Miss Fire, who immediately ignited her fireballs and went to work freeing Gemini from the marshmallow cast holding him in place.

"Aye," said Hawk, tossing his bow to the side and hefting his trusty sword and shield. He stood between the group and the angry Candemon in a defensive stance.

Wan-Wan's paws returned to their normal state, and the mechanical Akita bounded to Gemini as the boy got to his feet. Gemini shook off the fear he had at facing the Candemon alone and felt a renewed strength with his friends surrounding him.

"Where is Jimbob?" asked Miss Fire.

Gemini pointed to the marshmallow-encased eggplant near Roy G. Biv's throne in the center of Taffy Towers.

"Is it okay if I leave him there for a while?"

Gemini laughed and nodded his assent. He looked over Hawk's shoulder at the Candemon. The creature's face was contorted into a strange mixture of anger and confusion.

"Can't fight me alone, can you, hero?"

"I'll make you a deal," Gemini said. "You take off Roy's necklace and I'll fight you one-on-one."

The Candemon laughed. "I'm strong enough to defeat you all. Why would I risk my power to prove anything to you?"

"Pride? Honor?" suggested Hawk.

"A Candemon craves not these things!" spat the Candemon. It raised its arms to the crystal necklace and pointed it at the heroes. A wave of concentrated light shot out of the centermost crystal, a diamond, and flew toward the group. Hawk placed his shield in front of the light but it went straight through the barrier, singeing his shoulder but otherwise not hitting anyone.

"Hawk!" Gemini cried out while running to the knight's side.

"Just a flesh wound," Hawk declared.

"We need to get that necklace," Gemini said. He waved for Wan-Wan and Miss Fire to come closer. He lowered his voice and laid out his plan. "Wan-Wan and Miss Fire, you need to try to melt the Candemon's legs so it can't move. Hawk, try to get around behind it. I will take its attention from the front."

The four friends moved to prepare their assault on the Candemon, who was smiling its crooked hard-candy smile while playing with Roy's necklace.

"How much power do you really think you have?" Gemini asked the Candemon.

"The power of an Original."

Gemini shrugged his shoulders. "Big deal. Like that's so hard to get."

The Candemon glared at Gemini, the orange and blue hard candies that were his eyes molded into some sort of squint. Gemini reached behind his back into C-space and pulled out the eye of

Gumthulu to show to the Candemon. The Candemon's eyes widened at the sight of it, while Wan-Wan, Hawk, and Miss Fire began to flank the creature.

"I have here the eye of Gumthulu, an Original more powerful than Roy G. Biv. It contains all of the power of despair and evil and is much stronger than that necklace you have there."

A drip of saliva dropped from the side of the Candemon's twisted mouth. Gemini could tell that he was striking a nerve with the candy creature and pressed harder.

"How would you like to trade?" Gemini walked closer to the Candemon, holding the giant red gumball eye out in front of him. "You give me the necklace and I give you the eye. Light for Dark. Hope for Despair. I think this power is much more fitting for you, don't you?"

"How did you get the eye?" the Candemon suddenly asked, growing wary. "Gumthulu sleeps below this island and has not been awake in ages."

"The talking eggplant that you sprayed with marshmallow woke him and took the eye while we snuck onto the island through the Cave of Despair," Gemini explained honestly.

"Why don't I just take it from you?" the Candemon.

"Because I have a more powerful weapon and I am an Outsider, by default more powerful than you to begin with. There is no way you can win." Gemini smirked. "Maybe I should ask why I just don't take the necklace from you?"

"Why don't you?"

"Because . . . because . . . NOW!"

On his cue, Miss Fire shot fireballs from one side of the Candemon while Wan-Wan spewed flames from his mouth. The Candemon's chocolate-bar legs began melting almost immediately. While the creature was stunned, Hawk ran in behind and swiped at the crystal necklace with his sword. The necklace's string fell free, and the crystals clattered to the ground. Gemini dropped the eye of Gumthulu and scooped up the necklace.

The Candemon screamed in pain and anger as the flames stopped, leaving its legs partially melted and its powerful necklace removed.

"You tricked me!" it cried out.

Gemini shrugged his shoulders. "And you shouldn't even exist anymore." Gemini stepped over the molten chocolate of the Candemon's legs and stood in front of the creature. "Should you?"

The gold glowing from within the Candemon's gummy bear stomach shone brighter, and the tinkling noise became louder. Gemini thrust his hand into the gummy bear and removed the golden glowing object.

Immediately, the Candemon began to fall to dust and drift away. Gemini opened his hand, and the golden orb he was holding flew into the air, taking the shape of woman. Her face was not clear, but Gemini felt she was smiling.

"Thank you, Gemini," she said in an angelic voice. "Thank you for freeing me from that thing."

"You're welcome . . ." Gemini searched but did not know what to call the woman.

"My name was Eleanor. I heard what you were searching for, and I know where Shadowy Figure has made a home."

Gemini's eyes lit up. He was so caught up in the fight against the Candemon that he nearly forgot who he really was trying to defeat. "How? Where?"

"I knew everything that the Candemon knew. I was with him when he made a deal with Shadowy Figure. The Figure has created his own section of Toonopolis just through Gothicville. He has called it Shadowlands."

"Created his own section? Is that possible?"

"You just destroyed a candy creature, freeing the essence of a human that was trapped inside.

Candy Island

How could you question if anything is possible here?" Eleanor's essence laughed. "Go to Gothicville and you will find his Shadowlands just past the Sea of Vampires."

The golden form began to dissipate in the air. Gemini smiled as the woman's essence was freed to return to wherever it is that essences go. He watched her disappear then turned to his friends. Hawk had just roused Roy G. Biv from his stupor. Gemini picked up the crystal necklace and offered it to the gnome.

"You missed the fight," Gemini joked. "Here, I believe these are yours."

Roy smiled widely as he took the necklace from Gemini's hands. He quickly fastened it around his neck and leapt to his feet with more energy than Gemini had seen from the gnome since he first met him.

"Thank you, thank you, thank you," he mumbled as fast as he could. He then noticed Hawk, Miss Fire, and Wan-Wan. "You guys made it!"

"We said we would follow Sir Gemini to the ends of Toonopolis, did we not?" Hawk said with a smile.

"Did you come through the sewers?"

"Actually," Miss Fire answered, "we flew. When we realized that Wan-Wan had a rocket mode we left the sewers and flew over the ocean. We would have gotten here sooner but we needed the help of the cloud people to find the island."

"Cloud people?" asked Gemini.

"That's a whole different story involving a unicorn and a pirate, but I'm just glad we made it in time to help."

"Now what?" Roy asked.

"Maybe someone should get Jimbob out of that marshmallow," Gemini suggested.

"Do we have to?" Miss Fire joked.

Gemini glared at her, forcing her to grumble and walk to the marshmallowed eggplant. As she began to melt the white candy fluff, Gemini quickly filled Roy G. Biv in on the information given by the Candemon's creator regarding Shadowy Figure's whereabouts.

"Will you come with us to Gothicville?" Gemini asked Roy.

"I would love to," he said, "but I can't. King Ochopatas is still trapped somewhere on the island, and I have to set things straight here." Gemini frowned. "But I will still help you!"

Roy fingered his necklace and yanked on the diamond-shaped centerpiece, breaking it off. He handed it to Gemini with a smile.

Candy Island

"If you find yourself in a place without hope, the crystal will help you out of it."

"YEOUCH!" screamed Jimbob from outside the conversation. He sprinted past Gemini with his stem on fire and ran in circles until Wan-Wan shot fire-retardant foam at him. Jimbob blew the white foam away from his mouth.

"Oops," said Miss Fire.

"She did that on purpose!" Jimbob complained. He then looked around, slowly realizing that the Candemon was gone and their three other traveling companions had returned. "Did I miss something?"

Gemini slapped himself in the face with his palm and groaned. He filled in Jimbob on the fight with the Candemon and Eleanor's message. He retrieved the eye of Gumthulu and placed it back into C-space for Jimbob. Gemini then tucked the gnome's diamond crystal into the cargo pocket of his fuchsia pants and said good-bye to the Roy G. Biv.

His last view of Candy Island was from the back of Wan-Wan's rocket form. Alongside him were Jimbob, Miss Fire, and Hawk. They discussed their respective adventures since splitting up in the Toonopolis sewers. The company flew over Jellybean Jungle and Licorice Lagoon, heading toward Gothicville and, by extension, the Shadowlands created by Shadowy Figure.

Agent Log: Project Gemini
Entry Number: 19
Date: August 19

The widespread cases of Imagination
Deficit Disorder seemed to have slowed
down a bit but are not completely resolved.
The operative clearly is no longer
following the hit list that we prepared for
him while he was in the Tooniverse. This
has become quite an inconvenience, as my
superiors, while pragmatic, are not
entirely patient men. If it were not for the
initial glorious success of the program, I
am certain that my funding would already
have been cut.

In another note, Dr. Kraft has finally
discovered a section of Dr. Grenk's notes
that he had not shared with the rest of the
class. In a hidden folder on Grenk's
computer, Viktor found an entire series of
logs referring to what Dr. Grenk called

"subconscious meditation." It is a series of deep mind exercises that Grenk seems to have been practicing on himself. I am not entirely sure if it is related to our Project Gemini and the Tooniverse. My training, though, has always led me to assume that everything is connected and to sort out the details from there.

I approached Dr. Grenk about the files, and he became very defensive. He claimed that they were simply methods he had been using to deal with the stress of his recent divorce and his fears for his son inside Toonopolis. When I reminded him that he has had a few opportunities to remove his son from the Tooniverse, he simply stated that he feared removing Jacob's essence more than he feared leaving it inside the cartoon world.

His double-talking vexes me. My patience, like that of my superiors, is wearing thin. I have decided to practice some of these subconscious meditations myself and see what type of effect they have on me. If it turns out that he has not been, as I've worried, entirely forthcoming, it may be time to separate him from our project and continue with Dr. Kraft leading the research from now on.

Special Agent Mimic
August 19

Chapter Sixteen

Gothicville

Gemini's first thought as Wan-Wan flew them over the entranceway to Gothicville was that this section of Toonopolis looked like the result of a Wes Craven/Tim Burton brainstorming session. The only word he could come up with to describe the village was "creepy." Wan-Wan landed in one of the numerous cemeteries that filled Gothicville. Gemini, Miss Fire, Jimbob the Talking Eggplant, and Hawk slid off the robotic Akita.

Gemini looked around the cemetery and was amazed that even the individual blades of grass bent in such a crooked way that they oozed creepiness. The only sound he could hear was a soft breeze whispering through leafless trees. Most of the tombstones in the cemetery were illegible and half of the graves were either unfinished or, Gemini worried, recently evacuated.

A human skeleton, twirling in the wind, hung from one of the twisted, bare trees. Gemini shivered as his friends circled around.

"I want to go back to the Mother Nature throw-up place," whined Jimbob.

"Why are you such a crybaby?" asked Miss Fire.

Gemini's mind wandered from the constant sniping between Miss Fire and Jimbob. He looked up at the full moon partially obscured by thin wisps of clouds, and he realized that this was the first section of Toonopolis he had visited where it was nighttime. He sensed that he was very close to Shadowy Figure, and the anticipation of a final confrontation struck him.

"Shh," Gemini suddenly called to his bickering companions.

Jimbob and Miss Fire halted their argument. Hawk approached Gemini and knelt by his side. "What is it, m'lord?"

"I feel Shadowy Figure."

"I don't feel anything except creeped out," declared the eggplant. "What do you mean you 'feel' him?"

Gemini closed his eyes. "I feel a pull, like a magnet. I felt it before, when we were in Camenot, but I didn't know what it was. I know what it is now. I am drawn to Shadowy Figure. Eleanor was right; he's close. We need to find the Sea of Vampires."

"Oi," said a voice in a strong British accent.

Gemini looked around to try to find the source of the voice. He looked at Hawk, who shrugged his shoulders. Miss Fire and Jimbob looked around, and Wan-Wan barked and ran to the skeleton hanging from the tree. He sniffed at the dangling skeleton's foot and whimpered.

"'Allo, 'allo, pup," it said.

Wan-Wan yelped and snatched one of the feet in his jaws, yanking it off. He ran over to Gemini and dropped it on the ground.

"Now ain't that a fine how-do-ya-do."

"Bad Wan-Wan," Gemini said as he picked up the skeleton's foot. He walked to the skeleton's side and looked up at him. "Sorry about that. What are you doing up there?"

"Jus' hanging around." The skeleton laughed at his own joke, his jaw chattering as he did so.

Gemini handed him his foot, and the skeleton reconnected it to his ankle with a sickening, crackling sound.

"I am Gemini–"

"Roight," the skeleton interrupted. "All of us in Gothicville knows who you are, boy. That Shadowy Figure bloke told us all to keep an eye out for ya. I told him my eyes was already out." He laughed again, but it sounded a little forced. Gemini sensed fear in the skeleton when he began talking about Shadowy Figure. "The name's Nigel, by the way."

"So, Nigel," Jimbob started, "Shadowy Figure told you to look out for Gemini? Why?"

"He threatened to pureblack the entire village if we didn't make sure Gemini found his way to Shadowlands. We heard about the other sections of Toonopolis that he attacked. That guy is bad juju."

"Fortunately," Gemini said, "we are here to get to the Shadowlands so it won't be a problem for you. How do we get to the Sea of Vampires?"

Nigel turned his head to an unnatural angle and looked out past the cemetery. He pointed a skeletal finger toward a bridge in the distance. "Just over that bridge is the Sea."

"This place looks pretty dead," said Jimbob. He giggled a bit after he realized his pun. "Where is everyone?"

"Shadowy Figure has us all pretty spooked," Nigel replied with a pun of his own. "You won't be likely to meet up with anyone else here."

"Why not?" asked Gemini.

"Shadowy Figure's pretty scary, kid. We don't know what you did to make him so angry at you, but we're not like to find out any time soon."

Gemini nodded at Nigel. "Thanks."

"Sure thing. Not that I had any other plans, you see."

Gemini and his friends left the cemetery with Nigel the skeleton laughing awkwardly again. He walked down a main path in Gothicville and could feel eyes looking at him through windows and slightly opened doors. Gemini felt like he was in a bad episode of Scooby-Doo.

"Ironic that people in this creepy village should be scared of anything," Miss Fire said to no one specifically.

"Aye," Hawk agreed, his hand on the hilt of his sword. He seemed prepared to defend them at any moment.

After a few nondescript houses, they reached the bridge and a small house set against the side its

side. A sign was posted in front of it that read
"Don't Feed The Trolls." Gemini shook his head.

"What?" asked Jimbob.

Gemini pointed to the sign. "Wouldn't trolls be
out of place here? I mean, they're not really gothic
or creepy. They seem like they'd fit better in
Adventure Realm or Camenot."

"Unless . . ." Jimbob began.

"You're all probably fat, and I could beat you
all up!" cried a voice from under the bridge.

"Crap," said Jimbob.

"What is it?" asked Miss Fire.

"An Internet troll."

A small creature leapt from under the bridge
onto the pathway at the base of it. Gemini saw a
teenager about his own age wearing a T-shirt
decorated with a frowning yellow face. He had
greasy black hair, fingernails that were painted
black, looked as though he might have been crying.

"You're all ugly and stupid," said the troll.

Gemini stared at it. "Are you the grumpy old
troll that lives under the bridge?"

The troll's eyes lit up at Gemini's reaction.
"No, Dora, I live with your mom."

Gemini was visibly angered by the reference to
his mother. Jimbob hopped over to him and

placed a purple hand on Gemini's arm. "Calm down, Gemini."

"Um, maybe we should kill it."

"Internet trolls can't be killed," Jimbob said. "The only way to defeat them is to ignore them. If you try to fight Internet trolls, they multiply."

"So, all we have to do is just walk past it and not respond?" asked Gemini.

"Pretty much."

"Well, that's easy enough."

Gemini shrugged his shoulders and led his group past the Internet troll and onto the bridge. As Miss Fire walked past, Gemini heard the troll mumble, "Hey, woman, go back to the kitchen and make me a sandwich."

Miss Fire's eyes flared. Before Gemini could say anything, the Internet troll was on fire from one of her blasts. She looked satisfied with herself and continued walking over the bridge. Gemini watched in horror over Miss Fire's shoulder as the flames dissipated and two identical trolls were left standing on the bridge.

"Miss Fire, run!" cried Gemini.

Miss Fire turned around and saw that her attack had only created a second troll. She broke into a run, catching up with Gemini and the others on the opposite side of the bridge. Gemini couldn't exactly make out what the two trolls were saying but he heard plenty of nasty and inappropriate words as they left the bridge.

"That was interesting," said Hawk. "What is the Internet?"

Gemini and Jimbob looked at each other in a you-take-this-one moment, then they each held out a fist and counted, "One, Two, Three, Shoot." Gemini held his hand flat, and Jimbob's was a fist.

"Paper beats rock," Gemini declared.

"Well, Hawk," Jimbob said, "the Internet is basically a bunch of computers that are connected together. It has led to an abundance of information being easily accessible to anyone with a computer. It also has allowed people to be anonymous and feel that they can say whatever they want to anyone without any fear of repercussions. This is where Internet trolls were born."

Hawk nodded his head as Jimbob spoke. He took in all the information and then asked, "What is a computer?"

"I'll explain later, Hawk," said Miss Fire. Jimbob thanked her with his eyes for saving him from a longer explanation.

"Yes, m'lady."

Gemini got his team back on track as they walked away from the Internet troll's bridge. He could hear a slight lapping of water in the darkness in front of him, and an occasional hissing coming from the same direction. They continued walking toward the sound, and Gemini was amazed at what he saw.

"Holy Toonopolis," cried Jimbob. "I didn't realize that the Sea of Vampires was literal."

Gemini had expected to see a normal body of water that the Gothicville residents simply called the Sea of Vampires. He was not prepared for the fact that the water was actually obscured with countless vampire bodies. They ebbed and flowed with the waves, making it seem as though the sea itself was actually made of vampires instead of water.

"I've been waiting for you," said an elderly female voice in front of them. An old woman lifted her head and glared at Gemini. He hadn't noticed her because she wore a black cloak that blended in with the Sea of Vampires behind her.

"Who are you?"

"I am Lilith, governess of Gothicville," said the ancient woman. "I am to provide you with passage to the Shadowlands."

"You all seemed to give into Shadowy Figure pretty easily," declared Gemini. "I would think you would have put up a fight."

"Because we're scary creatures? Don't let our outward appearance fool you; we are very much into saving our own skin, regardless of who we have to sacrifice."

"Oh, so you're cowards," Jimbob observed.

"Pretty much," Lilith agreed without an argument.

"I could relate to that," he said with a nod, "before I faced off with the evil Gumthulu in the Cave of Despair and stole his eye."

Lilith rolled her eyes at the story.

"No, really," Jimbob maintained.

"What's with the Sea of Vampires?" Gemini asked, changing the topic.

Lilith looked over her shoulder at the sloshing body of water filled with vampire bodies. "I'm pretty sure I don't have to explain to you how Toonopolis works, right? That creations are made by the thoughts of intelligent beings?"

"Yes, we know how Toonopolis works," Gemini said.

"You humans seem to have vampires on the brain. We have been inundated with tons of vampires for years upon years. We didn't know what to do with all of the vampires sent to us from Sorting Square, so we created the Sea of Vampires with them." She waved her hand at the sea behind her.

"So you're saying that so many humans have created vampire toons that there are enough to fill an entire sea?" asked Jimbob in shock.

"That is exactly what I am saying," Lilith muttered. "What is it with humans and their obsession with vampires?"

Jimbob shrugged his shoulders. "I blame Anne Rice."

"Who?" asked Gemini.

"Never mind."

"Anyway," said Gemini, "you said you were here to grant me passage to the Shadowlands. How is that supposed to happen when the Sea of Vampires is literally a sea filled with vampires?"

"On a boat, obviously," Lilith replied. She pulled a magic wand out of her black cloak and said a few words under her breath. A rowboat appeared on the shoreline of the Sea of Vampires. Gemini and crew made to get into the boat, but Lilith stopped them. "One more thing," the governess said.

"What?" asked Gemini.

"Shadowy Figure said you had to go to him alone."

"What?" Gemini repeated.

"He said he wanted a fair one-on-one fight and that you couldn't bring your friends with you."

Gemini fumed as he looked at his companions who had stuck with him on his journey. "Fine," he conceded and stepped toward the boat.

"Jacob, no!" cried Jimbob the Talking Eggplant.

Gemini froze and turned slowly toward Jimbob. At the sound of his real first name, he was stunned. No one in the Tooniverse knew his real name. He blinked at Jimbob, who was staring at Gemini with fear.

"What did you call me?" Gemini asked.

Jimbob looked around at everyone and then back to Gemini. He sighed. "I guess it's time to come clean, Jacob."

Gemini did not reply, glaring at the two-foot talking eggplant that had accompanied him since the Sorting Square.

"I am kind of your father."

Gemini laughed. "Okay, Darth," he said through his laughter. He only stopped laughing when he saw that Jimbob was not laughing along with him.

"I'm not kidding, Jacob," the eggplant said with a straight face. "Remember when I asked Roy G. Biv if anyone from Earth had done the opposite of what the Candemon did?"

Gemini nodded his head.

"I only asked that because I did it. I found a way to follow the thread from my subconscious into the Tooniverse. Imagine my surprise when I found out that my creation was Jimbob here, a character I used to draw in my notebooks in college when I was bored." The eggplant stifled a weak laugh.

Gemini felt he couldn't believe what he was hearing but also that his ability to disbelieve things was strongly hampered by his time in the Tooniverse. "So you've been here this whole time?" he asked.

"Yes and no," Jimbob replied. "That's why I said I was 'kind of' your father. I couldn't constantly be here or I'd lose my grip on my body on Earth. Your body is still attached to that infernal machine I created, and I don't know what the Agency would do if I was no longer there. I have been in and out of Jimbob's body since you first got into Toonopolis, making sure you were okay."

"Well," interrupted Miss Fire, "that explains why you seemed like you had two different people in that big purple head of yours."

"So you forced your way into Jimbob? You're no better than the Candemon," Gemini accused.

"No!" cried the eggplant. "When I first found out how to travel into Jimbob's body, we talked. I explained what was going on. I asked him to help me look out for you. He accepts me sharing his body in the Tooniverse. He's my creation, but he's also become my friend."

"Then you lied to me back in the Black Light District when I asked where you were from?" Gemini accused.

"Again, yes and no. Jimbob told you the truth."

Gemini thought it was odd to hear his eggplant companion refer to himself in the third-, or maybe it was fourth-, person. Gemini's father continued talking with Jimbob's voice. "He really was a wanderer in Toonopolis with no real home. I may have encouraged him to become a Tooniverse guide so he could be close to you, but he did not lie to you."

Gemini was silent. He sat down on the edge of the rowboat and looked at his companions. Hawk and Wan-Wan stayed away from the conversation; they seemed not sure what to make of it. Lilith played with her wand. After her one comment, Miss Fire backed off to confer with Hawk.

"Jacob, I am sorry," was all Jimbob could say.

"For what?" Gemini spat out angrily. "For making Mom leave us? For volunteering me for this stupid project? For letting me think I was alone and abandoned inside this cartoon world, all the while checking up on me through that stupid eggplant? What are you sorry for, Dad?"

"I–"

"Or are you sorry that your experiment isn't going the way you planned? Are you sorry that something I did wrong, like losing my memories, is getting in the way of your research? All this time, I thought Jimbob was my friend and a companion. Now I find out that he was just a spy camera you used to get data for your research."

Jimbob lowered his eyes as Gemini stood up and hopped into the boat, which magically moved into the Sea of Vampires and began to drift away from the shore.

"I hate you," Gemini mumbled out loud. The hurt look on Jimbob's face let Gemini know that his father heard him. The eggplant slouched to the ground as Gemini drifted farther away from the shoreline.

"I can't believe him," he said to himself with tears in his eyes. He looked over the side of the boat at the bodies of the vampires that he was cleaving through. He tried to find his own reflection in the sea but there were too many vampires.

Gemini was so focused on his anger that he didn't see the arms of the vampire that reached up and grabbed him. Before he could fight back, the vampire dragged him out of the boat and into the sea. The Sea of Vampires engulfed him, and it wasn't long before Gemini's eyes rolled back into his head and he passed out.

Chapter Seventeen

Mindstate

Gemini opened his eyes and looked around. He could see only darkness in nearly every direction. He rubbed his eyes and saw a very faint light a distance ahead of him. The young man tried to remember what had happened before he opened his eyes and recalled that he'd taken a mystical rowboat to sail across the Sea of Vampires. His last thought was that he was drowning.

He waved his arms in the air, trying to feel if he was underwater. He felt virtually no resistance, so he guessed that he was not submerged in the Sea of Vampires. He felt around his body for any damages, but as far as he could tell, he was completely intact. Without any other choices, he began walking toward the light he could see.

He could not determine what type of surface he was on. It felt like solid ground, but there were no definitive markers between ground or sky or anything else. He felt like he was walking inside a black bubble. The light grew closer more quickly than he imagined was possible. His experiences so far in the Tooniverse reminded him that its rules weren't even remotely the same as they were on Earth.

The light suddenly was directly in front of him and he was able to identify a campfire. Four cloaked figures sat around the fire, with two additional chairs empty. One of the figures motioned for Gemini to sit down in the nearest empty chair. He sat.

"Glad you could make it, Gemini," said the figure to his left in a very familiar voice. The cloaked figure lowered his hood, and Gemini was very surprised to see his own face staring back at him. The three remaining figures lowered their hoods, also revealing faces identical to Gemini's.

"What is this all about?" Gemini asked. "In my time in the Tooniverse, I've seen a lot of strange things, but never clones of myself."

"Allow me to explain," said the doppleganger who had motioned for him to sit down. He stood up and removed his black cloak. He was dressed the same as Gemini, with fuchsia pants and a lime green shirt. The pants were dress slacks, and the top was a button-down dress shirt. He also had on a fuchsia tie. "You aren't in the Tooniverse right now."

Gemini's face contorted in confusion. The remaining three clones stood up and removed their cloaks. They were all identical to Gemini, except that their clothing was slightly different. Looking counterclockwise around the circle, Gemini noticed the differences.

The second had fuchsia shorts, a lime shirt, and a lime/fuchsia beanie cap complete with propeller. The chair directly across from Gemini was empty. The copy across from the one with the tie was wearing a lime and fuchsia striped pajama singlet, complete with attached foot-coverings. The last one, to Gemini's right, was the only one wearing different colors, or at least, different shades than Gemini wore. His outfit was a muted purple and green but was otherwise identical to Gemini's.

Mindstate

Gemini let his mind soak in the group of Geminis around him. "Where am I, then?" he said.

"You're in Jacob's subconscious," the tie-wearing Gemini said.

"Who are you all?"

"The same as you; we're all parts of Jacob's personality." He pointed at himself. "I am the mature side." He pointed around the circle counterclockwise at each successive clone. "His silly side. His childish side. His serious side."

"So, what am I?" Gemini asked, baffled.

"The good side, obviously."

Gemini looked across at the empty chair. He realized that each of the personalities had their opposites sitting across from them—mature-childish, silly-serious, good . . .

"And bad, yes," said the mature one.

"How did you know what I was thinking?" asked Gemini.

"We're all part of the same subconscious, friend. By the way, I love that you and Bad have cool names now. The four of us have tried to come up with names but we definitely can't beat Gemini and–"

"No!" screamed Gemini.

The silly side of Jacob Grenk spoke for the first time. "Are you telling me that you haven't realized by now that Shadowy Figure is also part of Jacob's personality? Man, maybe you should switch chairs with pajama-boy over there."

"Now, Silly," said the copy to Gemini's right, "this is an important matter."

"Pfft," Silly said. "It's always important with you, Serious. I think this whole situation is hilarious."

"You would," Serious said.

"Serious, Silly, please. We have to get Good, I mean, Gemini, educated about what's going on," Mature said.

Gemini shook his head trying to force the information he was receiving to make sense. He hoped he was simply dreaming and would wake up. Then he remembered that he was likely at the bottom of the Sea of Vampires. Even if he was dreaming, he wasn't sure waking up was such a good idea.

"Look, Gemini, let me explain it simply. The six of us made up Jacob's subconscious. Every decision he made or thought he processed filtered through us. If he had a dumb idea, it usually came from Footsies over there."

"His name is Footsies?" asked Gemini.

"We used to call him Childish, but he decided he liked Footsies better," Serious responded.

"Got it."

Mature continued, "Anyway, we would all try to get our say, but every one of us had our days of control. Sometimes Silly won the arguments, sometimes I would win, et cetera. Ultimately, Jacob was balanced because we all were involved."

"So, what went wrong?"

"The Tooniverse went wrong. When someone goes insane, it's because one or more of his or her six personality parts stops working properly. In our case, Bad simply escaped and became his own entity. On Earth, that couldn't happen. In the Tooniverse, it could and did."

"And Shadowy Figure was born?"

"Exactly. And what's worse, he took most of Jacob's memories with him to try to be his own complete person. You got most of them back when the two of you met up in Adventure Realm, but he still has all of the training the Agency gave Jacob in the months leading up to Project Gemini."

"And," Serious added, "since then, you've been so overly dominant that you've completely taken over Jacob's essence in the Tooniverse. The four of us have become spectators."

"I, for one," said Silly, "have found watching it all very entertaining."

"How have I become dominant?" Gemini asked.

"Simple," Mature said, "without the bad side of Jacob's personality to balance out the good side, you had no opposition to doing the 'good' thing in every circumstance."

Serious continued for Mature, "Remember when you said you felt like only the angel showed up on your shoulder and never the devil?"

"Yeah. So, the devil was Shadowy Figure and was separated from me, I mean Jacob. And that kept us from having a balanced personality?"

Serious nodded. "And presto, Good becomes Gemini and runs the whole show. We've been trying to get your attention for a while, but we couldn't get through. It wasn't until you got so angry at Jacob's dad that we finally felt a weakness. I was able to get a hold of Jacob's essence long enough to get you here."

"I like pizza," said Footsies.

"I agree," Silly responded. Silly smiled and looked at Gemini. "Yeah, he doesn't say much. But when he does, whew, look out."

Gemini stared at Footsies, who smiled simply back at him. He shook his head and looked back to Serious. "So, me falling into the Sea of Vampires had nothing to do with this visit to Jacob's subconscious?"

"Just a coincidence. I guess I grabbed onto the anger so hard that you couldn't defend yourself from the vampires."

"Don't worry," said Mature. "You're in Toonopolis. You've already spent time living underwater, so you know you'll be fine."

Gemini soaked in the information, then felt his anger welling again. All five of the personalities seemed to share it, and the fire in front of them grew a little bit. His angry feelings toward Jacob's father or Jimbob or whatever he was pretending to be resurged.

"I've been thinking about this, Gemini," Mature said.

"You? Thinking? Shock!" replied Silly.

Mature ignored Silly's comments and continued, "I don't know that we should allow Jacob to be that mad at his father."

"Poop face," Footsies declared.

"I concur," Silly added.

"I have to admit, between the divorce and signing Jacob up for Project Gemini, he has been somewhat of a bad father. But then again, maybe we just don't have all the information."

Silly scoffed and Footsies blew a raspberry. Serious simply listened intently. Gemini mirrored Serious.

Mature continued, "Shadowy Figure took some memories with him. We don't know if Jacob volunteered for Project Gemini. We also don't know everything that happened between Jacob's parents. Maybe there were more problems than just his dad's work habits. We have to remember that even if all six of us were here, we would still only have Jacob's interpretation of events to work with."

"Okay, fine, so maybe Dr. Grenk isn't a complete jerk," Gemini conceded. "But he still left Jacob, all of us really, abandoned in the Tooniverse, all the while watching us through Jimbob but never helping us escape."

"I disagree," Mature said. "Hasn't Jimbob been with you the whole time? Hasn't he helped you gather information and even stood side-by-side with you, fighting to get to Shadowy Figure?"

"Yeah, but that was just so he could collect data for his experiment."

"Once again, we don't know if that's true. What has he said since the beginning? He doesn't know what would happen if Jacob's essence was removed from the Tooniverse if it wasn't complete." Gemini and the others nodded. Footsies didn't nod because he was busy chewing on one of his pajama-covered feet.

Mature continued, "Remember how the Master Sorter said you weren't complete? I think he sensed something important was missing. If Jacob's essence were returned to Earth without his bad side, he'd go insane. Maybe Dr. Grenk realized this and has been trying to complete Jacob's essence before getting him out."

Serious cleared his throat, drawing attention away from Mature. "But if he knew Shadowy Figure was Jacob's bad side, why has he allowed all of the delays and side-quests. He's even the one who suggested Jack Montana might be Shadowy Figure."

"I don't think he's known the whole time. He just knew Jacob was incomplete. I'm not sure he even knows now that the Figure is part of Jacob. But he doesn't have any other ideas, so he helped Gemini pursue the Figure relentlessly."

Gemini sighed. "This is all so crazy. This whole time I thought I was Jacob Grenk. Now I find out that I'm just part of him. I can see why Shadowy Figure doesn't want to come back. To be free and be your own master? It's an interesting idea."

"But it's not right. You, of us all, should know that. Remember your feelings about Rogues and that anomaly?" Mature asked. "They were unnatural, abnormal. You, being the good side, fought them to set things right."

"I, for one, loved Sir Goodypants," Silly interjected. "I want to party with that guy."

"The fact of the matter is," Mature said, "we all have a creator that set us up a certain way, for better or worse. Trying to break out of that is against nature and never ends well, no matter how much it might seem to the contrary. I'd rather be part of a whole than a whole with a broken mind, wouldn't you?"

"So," Gemini said, neither agreeing nor disagreeing with Jacob's mature side. "Now what?"

"We need to get Bad back into his seat," Serious said, "no matter how much he resists."

"And how do we do that?" Gemini asked.

"We have no idea," Mature admitted.

"Battle!" shouted Footsies.

"Personally, I suggest you challenge him to a game of Battleship," Silly said. "Nothing settles life-or-death cases of subconscious personality wars like a good game of Battleship."

"Hungry Hungry Hippos?" said Footsies.

"As I said," Mature began, sounding annoyed, "we don't know how. We just know we need to be complete. Then we need to get back to Earth before we fracture again. I think there's a reason that Outsiders go insane here. If personality fragments can gain a physical form because of the lack of limitations in the Tooniverse, how many Outsider minds can possibly stay complete here?"

Gemini thought about Jack Montana, the Outsider who ran Toonopolis Fighting World and was attempting to start a frozen yogurt chain. He tried to figure out which part of his mind was broken. He presumed either Serious or Mature, because Childish and Silly definitely seemed to dominate him.

"Also," Mature continued, "we have to remember the destruction Bad has caused. With him absorbing countless creations, he's been damaging the minds of numerous people on Earth and who knows where else. We need to stop him. Don't you agree, Good?"

Gemini nodded. "You're pretty smart, Mature. Jacob is lucky to have you."

"Well, Jacob has been through a lot in his short life. Most teenagers are dominated by those two," he said, pointing to Silly and Footsies. "Jacob has had to rely more on Serious and me."

"I see. So, now I have to go back, defeat Shadowy Figure, put our mind back together, and get us out of the Tooniverse?" Gemini asked.

"That's about right," Serious said.

"Oh joy," Gemini said, getting to his feet. He looked around at his doppelgangers and sighed. "I guess it has to be me, right?"

"You're Bad's opposite, the only of us who would be able to defeat him," Mature answered.

"I figured as much," Gemini said. He looked at the darkness surrounding the six chairs and the fire. "How do I get out of here?"

Mature stood up, but Silly jumped out of his chair faster. He held up his hand to Mature and said, "I got this." He swirled his hand at Gemini, motioning for him to turn his back toward Silly. "Go get 'em, tiger," Silly said as he smacked Gemini on the butt. "Good game," he added.

Gemini was confused at what Silly was trying to do, then he felt himself lifting into the air. He looked down at the fire with the four remaining parts of Jacob Grenk's personality staring up at him, waving and giving him thumbs-up signs.

Gemini rose into the air until he felt a strong tug on his body. A faint light was above him, and he was pulled toward it. He took a deep breath and allowed the force to take hold of him. He had one final look at the speck of light below him that he knew held two remaining chairs that he needed to fill with himself and Shadowy Figure. Jacob Grenk's good side entered the light above him headfirst.

Chapter Eighteen

Shadowlands

Gemini coughed and sputtered as he awoke. He spit water and pointy vampire teeth onto the ground while struggling to get to his hands and knees. His hands gripped the sand as he evacuated his stomach of contents from the Sea of Vampires. It took him a moment to even realize that he was on dry land.

He opened his eyes and looked at the black sand underneath him, then he picked up a handful and was shocked to see that each grain of sand looked like a tiny little shadow or ball of smoke. The entire beach was full of this shadow-sand. He lifted his head and saw that everything in his vision was made of wisps of shadows. He saw a shadowy palm tree complete with shadowy coconuts. Much like Shadowy Figure, creator of the Shadowlands, everything had a vague sense of familiarity, cloaked with smoke and shadow, making their forms incomplete and their boundaries hazy.

He got to his feet and shook his head, trying to free himself of the sand on the outside and the cobwebs on the inside. The visit to his own subconscious was the most surreal thing he had experienced since entering the Tooniverse, which was a pretty strong statement considering how odd the whole adventure had been up to that point.

Gemini brushed the flecks of shadow-sand from his clothing and mentally prepared himself for the inevitable meeting with Shadowy Figure. The landscape on the shadow-beach was hard to follow. He could see indistinct lines between trees, the ground, and even the sky. He felt like it was one of those three dimensional visual pictures, where if you stared at it long enough you could make out the sailboat in the dots.

His eyes adjusted to the limited light of the Shadowlands, and he noticed a path between two of the trees lining the beach. Seeing no other options, Gemini walked across the black beach to the pathway. He paused between the two trees

Shadowlands

flanking either side of the path and gazed at the darkness ahead of him.

"WHOOOAAAA!" came a quickly descending shout from above.

Gemini looked up and saw a dark purple shape falling through the black sky. He had to squint to make out the object. When he saw the wide eyes and broad white mouth, he knew it was Jimbob the Talking Eggplant. His purple Toonopolis guide hit the ground, sending a shower of the shadow-sand into the air. Jimbob quickly bounced upright as the sand cascaded around him.

Jimbob looked up to the sky and said, "Well, that was not fun."

Gemini was once again flooded with emotions. When he first entered the boat to sail the Sea of Vampires, he was enraged at Jimbob for seemingly deceiving him. After his visit to Jacob's subconscious, he was willing to consider that his father might not have abandoned him. After all, Jimbob did just fall from the sky onto the Shadowlands beach. That had to mean something.

"Have a nice trip?" asked Gemini.

"See you next fall," Jimbob replied.

Gemini couldn't help but smile at an exchange that he and his father, both of whom were fairly clumsy on Earth, would often have. "Where did you come from?"

"We were trying to get into the Shadowlands to help you. There seems to be some sort of invisible barrier that kept Wan-Wan from flying us into Shadowy Figure's territory."

"But you're here," Gemini pointed out.

Jimbob smiled. "As we flew over, I bravely jumped off Wan-Wan to see if I could make it through."

Gemini narrowed his eyes at the talking eggplant. "Oh really?"

Jimbob opened his eyes wide. "Yes! I did. Very bravely, I would say."

"Mm-hmm."

Jimbob looked down at the ground sheepishly and finally admitted, "Okay, I fell off. Happy?"

"Did it hurt?"

"A little."

"Then, yes, I'm happy."

Jimbob looked hurt but resigned to Gemini's feelings toward him. Gemini watched Jimbob take in the strangeness of the scenery of Shadowy Figure's Shadowlands.

"Are the others coming?" Gemini asked.

Jimbob shook his head. "They can't get through the barrier. That witch in Gothicville said that Shadowy Figure put up a protective wall against any threat to him, except you."

"Then how did you get in?"

Jimbob shrugged and smiled. "I guess he doesn't see me as a threat." Gemini then saw Jimbob's smile falter a bit. "Are we going to pretend you don't know who I am, son?"

"I'm not your son," Gemini replied.

Jimbob stood frozen, as though he were having a heart attack. Gemini suddenly wondered if a cartoon eggplant would have a heart. He allowed the shock of his blunt statement to set in for a moment. During the pause, he realized how absolutely silent the Shadowlands were. He couldn't hear the slightest noise as he stood on the border between the beach and the trees.

He then broke the silence and explained to Jimbob/James Grenk the details of his conversation with the other segments of Jacob Grenk's personality. Jimbob seemed shocked at the revelation that Shadowy Figure was actually Jacob's bad side manifested in a physical form. Gemini took this to mean that Jacob's father didn't know who or what Shadowy Figure truly was.

"That explains a lot," Jimbob said. There was another moment of silence as the two pondered each other. "So," he said, leaving the word hanging in the air.

Gemini smiled. "I'm about to head into a fight with a being that is purely bad and has all of the memories of the training that the Agency gave Jacob when we were whole. I could really use my guide with me."

Jimbob returned the smile.

"Whoever we really are," Gemini said, "we can still be Gemini and Jimbob the Talking Eggplant going on one more adventure, right?"

The eggplant nodded his head happily and picked up a pile of the black sand at his feet, molded it into a circle, and poked a hole in the center. Gemini wrinkled his forehead at him. Jimbob held up his creation to Gemini and declared, "Look, a shadonut."

Gemini laughed and swatted the shadonut out of Jimbob's hands. "Now that's the Jimbob I remember. Shall we?"

He offered his elbow to Jimbob, who took it readily. The boy and the eggplant skipped side-by-side into the shadowy forest where the path wound through. The two of them whistled a cheery tune as they skipped, breaking the dense silence with their ironically happy song.

Gemini and Jimbob emerged from the shadow forest and faced a dark fortress. The black building looked like a cross between a castle and a prison. A chain fence with black barbed wire running along the top protected the exterior. Just past the fence was a deep moat. Gemini could see shadowy creatures moving in the dark water but could not make out what they were.

"Such an inviting place," said Jimbob.

On the other side of the moat stood the actual building. It appeared to be made out of black bricks. The walls were fairly low, and a single tower stood in the center. Even though everything was dark, Gemini felt he could see better than he should. He chalked it up to the benefit of being in a cartoon world.

"One guess where Shadowy Figure is," Gemini said, pointing to the tall tower in the center of the black-bricked structure, surprised to see colorful lights coming from the sole window at the top of the tower.

Jimbob nodded to Gemini and pulled out a fake mustache and a pizza box from C-space. "Disguise time?"

Gemini smiled, despite how nervous he felt about his impending confrontation with Jacob Grenk's bad side. He shook his head and said, "I don't think it'll work."

Jimbob frowned and put his pizza box down. "Can I still wear the mustache?"

"If you want."

The simple smile on Jimbob's face lightened Gemini's mood. They left the base of the trees and walked toward the fence to figure out a way inside. Gemini looked in both directions and could not see an entrance anywhere. He sighed and leaned forward to rest against the fence.

"Whoa!" he said as he fell straight through the barrier, leaving a puff of black smoke behind him. A Gemini-shaped hole was left in the black chain as he fell. Jimbob hopped through it.

"Is this whole place made of shadows and smoke?" Gemini asked as he got to his feet.

Jimbob waved a purple hand through another portion of the fence. A cloud of smoke wafted into the air from the spot. "Yep," said Jimbob.

"So, none of this is real?"

Jimbob bounced up and down. "The ground is real enough. Maybe he only had enough strength to create some reality and some illusion."

"And it's up to us to figure out which is which?"

Jimbob shrugged.

"Joy," said Gemini.

Having passed the fence, Gemini looked over the moat. With a closer look, he thought that the creatures swarming in the black water looked like alligators or crocodiles.

"Shadowgators?" asked Jimbob, peering over the edge of the moat alongside Gemini.

Shadowlands

"Or Shadowdiles, I guess," Gemini proposed. "I'm not sure how to tell the difference."

"It has something to do with the teeth," Jimbob supplied.

"First, I'm not sure it really matters what they are. Second, I don't think I want to get close enough to examine their teeth."

"Agreed."

Gemini stepped away from the edge of the moat and looked across to the other side. Jimbob followed his lead. The boy looked at the eggplant and smiled.

"What?" Jimbob asked nervously.

"Gravity Effectiveness Displacement?" Gemini asked. He could see the fear in Jimbob's eyes. Gemini remembered that his purple companion fell while in the Toonopolis sewers during his last attempt at the cartoon trick of not falling while walking off a cliff. Luckily for Jimbob, the flying stink-cloud Poot was there to catch him.

"I'm really not very good at that, Gemini."

"Think we could jump it?" Gemini asked. Jimbob looked down at his lack of legs and rolled his eyes at Gemini. "Fine," Gemini said with a huff.

He reached behind him and began pulling out a long plank of wood. Jimbob's eyes widened as the plank just kept coming from the mystical C-space behind Gemini's back. When Gemini finally got to the end of the plank, it was long enough to span the moat. He set it down and placed one foot on it to test its strength.

"You couldn't have done that first?" asked Jimbob the Talking Eggplant.

Gemini shrugged and said, "Didn't think of it." He grinned. "You want to go first?"

Jimbob shook his head vehemently.

Gemini placed his other foot on the wooden plank and began to slowly make his way across to the other side. He traversed the moat with little effort and was happy when his feet were on the ground on the opposite shore. He motioned for Jimbob to follow.

"Stupid Shadowlands. I don't like this place," Jimbob mumbled as he began hopping across the plank. When he was halfway across, he made the mistake of looking over the edge. Gemini noticed that the shadowgators were all swarming under the plank and fighting with one another for position.

"I would suggest that you don't fall," Gemini said.

"You think?" shouted Jimbob. He stopped looking and quickly bounded his way across the plank. He didn't stop at the edge and crashed right into Gemini, taking both of them to the ground.

"Scared much?" Gemini mocked.

The two of them untangled from each other and turned away from the moat to look at the black brick wall of Shadowy Figure's fortress. Gemini gazed at the top of the tower again and could see a shape moving around amidst the color emanating from the upper window.

"What do you think he's doing up there?" Gemini asked.

"I have no idea," Jimbob admitted. "With all of this darkness around us, maybe he's trying to add color?"

"But where is he getting the color?"

"From the creations he absorbed, I bet."

Gemini shuddered at the thought of creations being used as coloring utensils. He took his eyes off the top of the shadowy tower and looked at the wall instead. It was at that time that he felt a sharp pain in his leg. He screamed and looked at the shadowgator that had bitten him. A quick survey amidst his pain and confusion showed that the wooden plank had slipped, giving the shadowgators a path to climb up out of the moat.

"Get off of me!" Gemini shouted and flailed his arms at the creature. "Jimbob, help!"

The talking eggplant leapt onto the shadowgator's back, only to realize that five more were impatiently waiting for their turn. A quick sweep of one of their tails sent Jimbob sprawling to the dark ground with a bruising thump.

Gemini fell over as the shadowgator attached to his foot began to roll. On his back, Gemini was free to use his other foot as a weapon and kicked the shadowgator in the snout. Instead of letting go, the gator bit down harder, forcing Gemini to close his eyes in pain. He didn't see the second and third gators jump onto him.

He felt the pressure of the shadowgators beginning to crush him. His arms were pinned down so he could not reach into C-space for any weapon that might help him. He could hear Jimbob struggling with a few of the gators too. Gemini closed his eyes tightly and felt overwhelmed and scared.

POOF!

Gemini heard a strange poofing sound and immediately felt the weight of the shadowgators lifted from his body. His left foot ached with pain from the gator's bite, but the gator itself was no longer there. He opened his eyes, expecting another attack. He was amazed that the gators were gone.

"Jimbob, are you okay? What happened?"

"The gators are gone," Jimbob answered.

"Thanks for the update, Captain Obvious. Where did they go?"

"I put them back in their hole," answered a raspy voice that gave Gemini a chill.

Gemini followed the voice and knew that he would find Shadowy Figure standing at the base of the brick wall.

"Quit the games, Bad. I know who we both are now."

The shadows and smoke that swirled around Shadowy Figure, ever obscuring his appearance, began to drift away. When it was gone, Gemini was looking at yet another version of himself. Instead of the lime and fuchsia colors, Shadowy Figure's clothes were forest green and royal purple. His hair was a dark auburn and even his skin was a darker shade of peach.

"I like my look better, Good," he said with a twisted grin. "It took you long enough to figure out what we are."

Gemini got to his feet, trying to keep his weight off the injured leg. "Why did you call off the shadowgators?"

"Shadowdiles, actually. Didn't you see their teeth?"

"No, sorry, I was too busy getting bitten by them."

"Fair enough," said Shadowy Figure with a little laugh. "I called them off because I need you intact before I absorb you and retrieve the rest of Jacob's memories and personality segments."

"What for?" asked Jimbob, who had been quietly observing the conversation between the two toons that looked like his son.

"I need the power of his complete Outsider mind if I am to fully take over Toonopolis, obviously. All of the creations I've absorbed only give me a little taste of power. Getting the rest of an Outsider would be like an all-you-can-eat buffet."

"If you destroy the rest of Jacob's personalities, you will destroy yourself too," Gemini declared, not really knowing if it was true. He felt the bluff had merit, however.

"I don't plan on destroying you. I'll just keep you trapped inside me. You met the Candemon, right?"

Gemini thought about the golden orb of the Candemon's creator, trapped inside the creation for countless years. He knew that he did not want to share that fate.

"You jerk," Jimbob cried.

"Yeah, first off, you need to shut up," Shadowy Figure said. He waved his hand at Jimbob, who was quickly engulfed in a pureblack orb.

Shadowlands

"Jimbob! Dad! No!" Gemini screamed and ran toward the small pureblack sphere that encompassed his companion/father.

Shadowy Figure's smug grin dropped momentarily when he realized what Gemini just said. "Did you say 'Dad'? That stupid eggplant is Jacob's father? That is priceless!" Shadowy Figure began laughing hysterically.

"Your father, too, Bad," Gemini pointed out while trying to punch and kick at the sphere.

"Distantly. I don't consider myself Jacob anymore. I'm something better. Besides, Jacob's father doesn't care about him, anyway. Or did you forget that he's the reason we're here in the first place? Maybe I *should* thank him!"

Gemini stopped pounding on the orb and reached quickly into C-space to get his trusty giant mallet. He stood in front of Shadowy Figure menacingly.

Shadowy Figure grinned. "Yeah, I don't think so."

He waved his hand, and Gemini was absorbed into darkness. Inside the pureblack sphere, Gemini could not hear or see anything. He had thought that the Shadowlands were filled with darkness and blackness, but he now knew what Roy G. Biv meant when he described pureblack.

Toonopolis: Gemini

He tested his limbs and felt that he could move, like he was trying to move his arms and legs through a swimming pool filled with caramel. He closed his eyes and opened them again, his vision being no different either way. He allowed a hint of despair to creep into his mind, fearing that he had come all this way to allow Shadowy Figure to win so easily.

He continued trying to move his arms, and his fingers brushed against something hard in his pocket. Gemini had a flash of memory hit him as soon as his fingers touched the object. He slowly moved his hand through the thick soupy blackness until he was able to reach the object inside.

He pulled it out and immediately felt lighter. A burst of rainbow colors jumped from the object, shattering the pureblack orb around him. He found himself sputtering on the ground next to Shadowy Figure, his nemesis looking completely shocked that Gemini was able to get out of the sphere.

"How in Toonopolis?" Shadowy Figure cried out.

Gemini held up the object that had saved his life—the diamond-shaped crystal from Roy G. Biv's necklace. Shadowy Figure thrust another pureblack sphere at Gemini but it simply deflected off the crystal in Gemini's hand.

"That blasted gnome," Jacob Grenk's bad side cursed. "And that stupid Candemon."

"Time to go back into Jacob's mind, Shadowy Figure," Gemini said calmly.

"Why? Wouldn't you rather just stay out? Be your own creation? Why would you want to go back to being part of a whole when you can be your own whole?"

"Because it's not right," Gemini answered.

"That's your argument? 'Because it's not right'?" Shadowy Figure spat.

Gemini shrugged and said, "It's how I operate. I'm the good side, remember? My job is to help Jacob and be a part of him." Feeling more confident while holding Roy G. Biv's crystal, Gemini took a step toward Shadowy Figure. "And so is yours."

"I won't go back," Shadowy Figure said. "I'd rather die than go back."

Gemini held up the crystal and willed some of the trapped light to escape. Beams of multicolored light shot in every direction. The brick walls of Shadowy Figure's fortress crumbled as the light touched them. The pureblack orb around Jimbob burst, freeing the eggplant from his captivity. Shadowy Figure cowered from the light.

"You don't have that choice," Gemini said to Shadowy Figure.

He willed more light to escape. As the walls and tower fell, ghosts of color escaped. Gemini could make out sea creatures that reminded him of Underwater City and some black-and-white creations from Grayscale Village. Tons of two-dimensional stick figures escaped as well. He realized that the light from Roy's crystal was freeing all of the absorbed creations. The cartoons took to the sky, making swirls of color as they traveled away from the Shadowlands and, Gemini guessed, back to where they belonged.

"Jacob! Gemini! Whatever!" Jimbob howled.

"What's wrong?" Gemini asked the hysterical vegetable.

"It's Agent Mimic of the Agency. He's about to remove you from the machine on Earth. You need to get complete before he pulls you out of the Tooniverse. We have no idea what will happen if you are incomplete."

Gemini tried to process the information Jimbob, AKA James Grenk, was throwing at him. He did not have memories of Jacob's time at the Agency, but he knew that Jacob's essence was in Toonopolis as an experiment run by the Agency. He also knew that Jimbob's creator, Jacob's father, was the scientist in charge of the project.

"Can't you stop him?" Gemini asked.

"He's insanely angry and much bigger than me. He knocked me to the ground. He found out about my method for tracing the thread back to my own creation without being in a coma. You need to finish this!"

Gemini's dark doppelganger swiftly kicked the diamond crystal out of Gemini's hand. Without the light to keep Shadowy Figure at bay, the bad side of Jacob Grenk's personality tackled Gemini to the ground. Light still emanated from the crystal haphazardly, causing portions of the Shadowlands to revert back to their original creations. Even parts of the ground were starting to vanish.

"SIR GEMINI!" a cry came from above.

Gemini looked up from his back over the shoulder of Shadowy Figure. He could see a descending Wan-Wan with Gemini's other two friends, Miss Fire and Hawk, on his back. He kicked Shadowy Figure in the stomach, sending him back to a portion of the Shadowlands ground that was still whole. Wan-Wan landed near Jimbob.

"What's going on?" asked Miss Fire. "Why are there two Geminis?"

"Too much to explain! How did you get through?"

"We followed the trail of the escaping toons," Miss Fire replied. "They cut a hole in the barrier, I guess."

The crystal continued spinning on the ground. The walls of Shadowy Figure's fortress now had gaping holes in it and continued crumbling and turning back into the creations that Shadowy Figure used to build his Shadowlands.

"Nooo!" screamed Jimbob.

Miss Fire and Hawk gazed at Jimbob, as if he were insane, which was not really abnormal. This time, though, it was because they did not know why he was screaming. Gemini frowned.

Shadowy Figure got to his feet laughing. "You feel that, Gemini? Earth is trying to pull us back. Jacob is trying to wake up but he can't."

"You need to get back together with us, Figure, or you will die along with us!" Gemini said, trying to appeal to Shadowy Figure's baser instincts of survival.

"I've had a taste of being my own master. I can't go back to being a part of one anymore. Good-bye, Gemini."

Shadowy Figure turned his back to Gemini, who was horrified to see his copy's face begin to pixelate. Gemini held up his own hands and watched the same thing begin to happen to his body. He looked at Jimbob and his other friends.

Shadowlands

They were becoming separated from Gemini and Shadowy Figure by the large chunks of the Shadowlands that were disappearing due to the blasts of light from Roy's crystal.

Finally, Gemini felt his entire body disperse while he watched the same thing happen to Shadowy Figure. As their bodies vanished, thin stretches of golden light streamed from them. The two wisps of light met in the air above where their bodies once stood. They merged into a golden orb and then morphed into a singular form of a teenage boy. The form floated above the rapidly vanishing Shadowlands.

Jacob Grenk's golden essence looked down upon his traveling companions: the robot dog from Animetown, the paladin from Camenot, and the superheroine from Supercity. He smiled at them.

Lastly, Jacob Grenk looked at Jimbob the Talking Eggplant, his father's cartoon creation, who had accompanied him since his journey began. He thought his father had abandoned him, then he came to realize that his father, through Jimbob, had risked everything, including his research, to follow Gemini to the end of his journey.

"I forgive you and I love you, dad," Gemini's essence said. He saw a purple tear fall from the corner of Jimbob's eye. Gemini's golden form began to dissipate in the air and he waved what was left of his formless arm to his friends. He felt a strange pull on his essence followed by a faint popping sound that was oddly familiar.

E p i l o g u e

Agent Log: Project Gemini
Entry Number: 22
Date: September 9

Unfortunately, I had to pull the plug on Project Gemini, and this will be my last entry on this particular project. I needed access to the data that only Jacob Grenk could give me as to what happened while he was in the Tooniverse. Dr. Grenk attempted to stop me, shouting craziness about his son being "incomplete" and not knowing what would happen when we tried to remove his essence from the Tooniverse.

I am not entirely sure what happened. I do know, however, that a lot of valuable data was potentially lost because Jacob Grenk did not emerge from his controlled coma when I shut down the machine. His body showed all signs of being alive; his respiratory, nervous, and circulatory systems all checked out on our monitors.

I left to file a report on the failure to retrieve the information within the subject's memory. I returned only to discover that both Dr. Grenk and his son's body were gone. I attempted to review the security cameras, but Grenk had disabled them. Before he shut them down, however, I saw that Jacob clearly had returned from the Tooniverse.

As of right now, I am unaware of their location. This is a minor issue that will be rectified shortly. I feel I should be sad about the loss of our first subject, but as the saying goes, one can't make an omelet without cracking a few eggs.

To use another cliché, when one door closes, another opens. In a previous entry, I referred to a series of notes that Dr. Grenk had on his computer about a method called "subconscious meditation." Through my own experimental usage of these methods, I found that Dr. Grenk had discovered a way of tracing the thread

Epilogue

connecting himself to his creation in Toonopolis. He was able to share his creation's body inside the Tooniverse.

This opens up an entirely new realm of possibilities far beyond sending a trained operative into the Tooniverse via Project Gemini. I was only able to hold onto the thread for a very short period of time, but I am sure that, with practice, I will be able to sustain myself inside the Tooniverse. I will certainly use this in my continued experimentation of Toonopolis-Earth interactions.

To close out Project Gemini, I must sadly report that the rampant cases of Imagination Deficit Disorder brought on by the actions of Jacob Grenk inside the Tooniverse all miraculously reversed themselves around the same time that I pulled the plug on Jacob's time in Toonopolis. This also included our target list that was so expertly incapacitated early in the project. My superiors in the Agency have expressed concern about this, but I assured them that the next step in

Project Gemini would surely produce even greater results.

To assuage their concerns, I told them a story about a creature that I had heard about while inside Toonopolis, a real unicorn that had bodily transmitted itself to Toonopolis using its magic. I briefed them on the legendary powers of the unicorn and assured them that this one was quite real and possessed magic that could be used to our advantage, if we could somehow "persuade" the beast to work for us.

With my newfound ability to operate both inside Toonopolis and on Earth simultaneously, I see no reason to send an unseasoned operative back inside. This time I will get my own hands dirty, so to speak.

Special Agent Mimic
September 9

Acknowledgements

I would like to thank all of my friends and family, especially my mother, for their support and encouragement. Thank you also to my two wonderful sons, who keep my mind young enough to explore my imagination every day.

Thanks to those who were brave enough to read through and critique the entire skeletal first draft: Ariel Baker, Nelson Diaz, and Elizabeth Mansure. Thanks to Jennifer Bruck for her help with design and font selection, not to mention her supportive fangirling.

Lastly, thanks to my editor, Dennis Billuni, for helping me to improve my writing without changing my voice.

About the Author

Author Photo By Julia Haggerty

Jeremy Rodden holds a Bachelor's degree in Religion and English Writing from La Salle University and a Master's in Education from Holy Family University. He worked briefly as a High School English teacher before becoming a full-time stay-at-home dad and author.

Follow his blog and learn more about the author and his works at www.toonopolis.com.

9 780983 425397